W9-CHB-405

HOLLY BENNETT

THE
WARRIOR'S
DAUGHTER

ORCA BOOK PUBLISHERS

Copyright © 2007 Holly Bennett

All rights reserved. No part of this publication may be reproduced
or transmitted in any form or by any means, electronic or mechanical, including
photocopying, recording or by any information storage and retrieval system now
known or to be invented, without permission in writing from the publisher.

Library and Archives Canada Cataloguing in Publication

Bennett, Holly, 1957-

The warrior's daughter / written by Holly Bennett.

ISBN 978-1-55143-607-4

I. Title.

PS8603.E62W37 2007   jC813'.6   C2006-906671-X

Summary: The daughter of Ulster's mightiest warrior must
find her own path through grief, pain and wonder.

First published in the United States 2007
Library of Congress Control Number: 2006938221

Orca Book Publishers gratefully acknowledges the support for its publishing programs provided by the following agencies: the Government of
Canada through the Book Publishing Industry Development Program and
the Canada Council for the Arts, and the Province of British Columbia
through the BC Arts Council and the Book Publishing Tax Credit.

Cover artwork, cover design, interior map: Cathy Maclean
Typesetting: Christine Toller
Author photo: Wayne Eardley

The author is grateful for the support of the Canada Council
for the Arts which enabled the research for this book.

In Canada: the United States:
PO Box 5626, Stn. B   PO Box 468
Victoria, BC   Canada   Custer, WA USA
V8R 6S4   98240-0468

www.orcabook.com
Printed and bound in Canada.

010 09 08 07 • 5 4 3 2 1

Acknowledgments

My special thanks are due first and foremost to storyteller, author, scholar and "legendary tour guide," Richard Marsh of Dublin, for showing me the locations where this story takes place, suggesting useful research sources, clarifying areas of confusion, proofreading my manuscript for technical errors and being an all-around goldmine of information. Any remaining errors are, of course, mine and not his.

Thanks also to:

Joanne Findon, Associate Professor of English Literature at Trent University and Ulster Cycle scholar, for advising me on the pronunciation and phonetic spelling of old Irish names;

Lady Augusta Gregory, for seeing the beauty and value of these ancient stories and first bringing them to the English-speaking public;

My editor, Sarah Harvey, for helping me find the right balance of modern and traditional narrative and holding my hand through the hard parts;

Cover illustrator, Cathy Maclean, for the three gorgeous covers she has designed for my stories;

My agent, Lynn Bennett;

And finally, thanks to my family for their whole-hearted support and above all to my husband, John, who bravely drove me all over Ireland in a standard-transmission car.

SERC LIBRARY

Contents

SERC LIBRARY

PREFACE

When I first stumbled across the ancient Irish sagas of Cuchulainn and his wife Emer, I fell instantly in love. Never had I read a traditional tale so full of emotional resonance, or peopled with such wonderful characters. And presumptuous though I knew it was to attempt an interpretation of another culture's myth, Cuchulainn and Emer preyed on my mind until it was useless to resist. Bolstering my nerve with the thought of my Irish great-grandparents, I plunged in.

These stories, dating from about the time of Christ, were first written down in Medieval Irish script in various versions and fragments starting from about the eighth century AD. Without the scholarship and dedication of the people who pieced them together and translated them into a coherent English narrative, they would have been forever beyond my reach. My heartfelt thanks, then, go to the two translators I relied on most heavily: Lady Augusta Gregory, who wrote her *Cuchulain of Muirthemne* in 1902, and Thomas Kinsella, who published *The Táin* in 1969.

Although Lady Gregory omitted some passages she thought her squeamish Victorian audience "would not be interested in," and has been accused of being over-flowery, her translation has a charming idiomatic voice that brought the characters of the Tain alive to me. I have borrowed her words for the dialogue in several places, and I hope she would take this as I intend it: as a tribute to the beauty of her speech and a way of bringing some feel of the "original" to the modern reader. Kinsella's more spare and muscular narrative has a classic epic tone and was a constant reminder to me that the Iron Age Celts (1000 BC–43 AD) did not inhabit the dreamy landscape of medieval chivalry that is familiar to most readers, but a tougher and lustier place altogether.

The characters in the *Cattle Raid of Cooley*—the *Táin Bó Cuailnge*—hurl themselves through life at a kind of fever pitch: no challenge unmet, no love denied, no risk too daunting, no oath refused. And then, having embraced their lives with such blazing passion, they give them up with the same reckless abandon, to the spear or the sword, to broken hearts or unbearable shame, even to the humiliation of a satirist's caustic tongue. They must have been short enough, those lives, and perhaps the final blaze of glory was after all a better way to end than the slow, painful onslaught of disease that was the likely alternative.

I loved these people, with their pride and their courage, their determination to burn bright rather than burn long. I hope you like them too.

A NOTE ON NAMES

What to do with all these Irish names? Too beautiful to replace with English versions, they are nevertheless a daunting mouthful for an Anglo reader and nearly impossible to pronounce correctly without coaching. I've settled on this solution: I've kept most names as I found them (usually the simplest of the available variants), and provided a pronunciation guide (Who's Who—and How to Say It, p. 224) that is no more than a rough approximation. But you know what? It's a story, and whatever pronunciation you hear in your own head will do just fine. Loo-ayn does not, to my ear, sound as pretty as Loo-in-ya, but my heroine, Luaine, will answer to either one.

In a couple of cases, I've replaced an Irish place name with a simpler spelling currently in use. If you go to Ireland today, you can visit the Cooley Hills, so I saw no need to puzzle the reader with "Cuailnge."

And finally, I have omitted the fadas, or accents, from all Irish words, since they are no help to a North American reader.

I am a raven that has no home; I am a boat going from wave to wave; I am a ship that has lost its rudder; I am the apple left on the tree; it is little I thought of falling from it; grief and sorrow will be with me from this time.

—Lady Augusta Gregory, *Cuchulain of Muirthemne*

Ireland at the time of Cuchulainn

PROLOGUE

It's true my father was a mighty man altogether.

Not all the stories they tell about him are true, of course, or not entirely. We are, after all, a people who love a good tale even better than a good fight, and I do not blame the bards for adding their own improvements to the history of the great Cuchulainn. Indeed, I am grateful, for in even the most fantastic details I find a true memory of the living man.

There are no stories about me, however—nor will there be, if Cathbad has his way. When those who knew me pass from this earth, the memory of my name will pass with them. Doubtless he is correct; Cathbad is counted wise among the druids, though like any man he has his own reasons for his advice.

And so I seek obscurity, at least for my old name. But there is enough of my father in me—and my mother too, for Emer was hardly one to shrink into the shadows!—to want my own story told, at least one time.

Will you listen and keep silent? It is my life I am trusting you with.

My name was Luaine.

PART I

CHAPTER 1
THE WARRIOR'S WRATH

The old white horse, usually so slow and patient, was frisky as a colt that day, and I was having a hard time to make him mind. Perhaps it was the rich breath of spring gone to his head; if truth be told, my own attention wandered away on the breeze more than once.

I was kicking him up from a trot to a canter when a sudden jolt catapulted me forward and my view was suddenly of muddy ground rather than blue sky and wattle fencing. Clutching with hands and knees, I managed to hang on to his neck—just. Completely unconcerned with the small person clinging upside down to his mane, the evil old nag cropped contentedly at the clump of vetch that had caught his eye.

Snorting with laughter, the stable master loped over to rescue me.

"Can you regain your seat, young miss, or will you and your horse be parting company?"

"Get me down, Niall!" It was a long way to the ground and an ugly landing at the end.

"That I will not. But I will show you how to get yourself down should this ever happen again. Though you would do better to keep control of your steed in the first place."

Strong hands supported me, guiding my head down beside the horse's neck and drawing my feet up and over in a somersault. To my surprise, I landed with a bump and a stagger but on my feet.

"Luaine!"

It was my mother, striding toward the paddock with my nurse fluttering behind. There was a controlled urgency to her voice that made it clear this was no time for protests or games. I looked to Niall.

"Go on, then," he said as he boosted me over the fence. "I'll take care of this old bugger."

My mother hurried to meet me. "Come along, Luaine, you can't stay out here." She held out her slim hand and pulled me up the steep path that led to our gate.

We were nearly across the yard before I managed to ask, "What is wrong, Ma?"

"I've just had word your father returns, and with the battle-frenzy still upon him. He scarce knows friend from foe while the red wrath drives him. It's inside and out of sight with you, now. I will come when it is safe for you to see him."

"Mistress," my nurse quavered, "should you not hide yourself here as well? Will you not be in danger also?"

"Don't be ridiculous." My mother stopped and turned to Tullia in genuine indignation. "I will greet my husband as is my duty and my privilege. He is no danger to me." She said this in utter confidence, and I understood suddenly that not only was she unafraid, she was glad of the challenge. There was honor and pride for her, in knowing how to gentle my father back to himself. "Tullia, you had best stay here with Luaine. My lord would not wish to strike off your head unawares."

Poor Tullia blanched at the reproof and drew me hastily into my mother's workroom. Tucked beside our main hall, the room was dominated by her great loom and cluttered with bags of fleece and bright skeins of wool. It was a room for women's arts and my father never went there.

As we sat silently in the room's darkest nook, I thought of the wild descriptions I had heard of my father in battle. How my eyes shone with excitement, and my mother's with pride, when he recounted his victories! All mighty warriors know the frenzy—the battle madness that gives them strength and reckless ferocity—but my father's, to hear tell, was truly terrifying. I shuddered as I tried to picture it: the fire flashing from his bared teeth, the spout of smoking blood rising out of his skull, the one eye sucked deep in his head while the other hung down over his cheek. A nightmare come to life.

Even at seven, I knew some of what was told was plain nonsense. How could a man be after fighting with his legs and feet turned backward in his skin? But the thought stole over me, when I heard the thunder of hoofbeats and the rumble of chariot wheels that heralded his arrival, to see for myself.

I bolted away from Tullia and scrambled up the ladder to the loft that ran right around the big circle of our house. Hurrying past the tidy storage areas for grain and herbs, sausages and hams, bedding and extra sleeping pallets, I made for the spot just above the door. Then I pulled out the small work knife I carried at my waist and began hacking at the roof thatch, not minding the damage I was causing or the scratches I suffered as I thrust my thin arms into the bundled reeds. It was dauntingly hard work—thatch, I discovered, is a lot tougher than you might think—and hot up there under the eaves. By the time I finally had a peephole carved out I was afraid it might be too late. But I crouched and put my eye to it nonetheless, and I caught my breath at the view that spread

out below me: a long sweep of thatch and then the crescent of
our yard, edged with the strong fence and heavy front gate, and
beyond that the plain of Muirthemne, green on green on green
to the very end of my sight.

≡

Up until that day I had never been afraid of my father. I saw but
little of him for he was often away, but he was always kindly and
fair-spoken to me. And then of course, he was so handsome.
Women adored him, and I suppose I was no exception. He had
a smile on him that poured over you so that you had to smile
back, just for the joy of seeing it. When he looked at you—*really*
looked at you—with approval or affection, you wanted to swim
forever in the dazzling blue light of his eyes.

He was young and boyish still, full of tricks and playfulness.
And if he had sometimes forgotten his strength and caused hurt
to his playmates as a boy on the field of Emain Macha, he never
did so with me. He would throw me high into the air—not some
little toss, it's looking down on the thatch of the roof I was—and
catch me as gently as if I were landing on a feather pillow. He
would take me up on his great gray horse and we would race across
the plain till the world streamed by me in a blur, and never did
it occur to me that I might fall. For my father himself had tamed
that horse, which nobody else could approach, and ridden him
without once losing his seat while The Gray bucked and fought
over all the provinces of Ireland. It must have alarmed my mother
when he began to play with me so, but no doubt she soon saw
that he kept care for me, for she did not speak against it.

She liked it better when he entertained us with his feats and
tricks, for then she could relax her mother's watchfulness. "Fetch

the apples," he would say with a wink, and I would run to the pantry and struggle to drag out the big basket of them, determined I would need no help. He would start to juggle, a few at first, then more and more until the air was thick with apples. And I would squirm and giggle in anticipation, for suddenly his sword would be out, and the apples falling in halves around us in a great pile, with none ever landing in one piece.

When we had done laughing and clapping, my mother would call for a servant girl. "Take these in to the cook. It's honeyed apples for everyone tonight!"

Ξ

I could have clung to that happy image of my father, and part of me did want to run back to my nurse's arms and stay a baby. But the stronger part of me needed to know. And so I ignored Tullia's fearful call, and I watched.

My mother stood entirely alone, a straight still figure. I thought she must be the most beautiful woman on earth, with her hair that gleamed bronze in the sunlight and the smooth white skin of her arms. Gold caught the light at her neck—the rich red gold, it was, that looked so fine with her hair.

Cuchulainn's chariot thundered over the plain with a din that made me cover my ears—oh, it was a brave sight, though, with the two great horses racing before it and the silver knives bristling from its wheels! Then it was my father, vaulting over the side before the horses could stop and striding up to the open gate where my mother waited. She bowed her head very deeply and did not move.

I was relieved to see his eyes both where they belonged. But on my soul, they were not the eyes I knew. Wild and bloodshot, they squinted at my mother as if he could barely see. With the gold gleaming on him and the stain of blood streaked over his body, his clothes rent as though he had burst out of them, he was the most fearsome thing I had seen in my short years. The face on him was dark with rage; his muscles rippled and clenched; the breath heaved out of his chest with a noise more like to a beast than a man. Indeed he seemed scarce able to speak as he wrestled to subdue the frenzy that rode him.

His sword was still unsheathed in his hand as he towered over my mother.

He will kill her, I remember thinking. He will give in to the pull of the sword. My heart knocked about in my chest like a weasel in a trap.

"Welcome, Cuchulainn, Lord of Muirthemne and Champion of Ulster." My mother had very slowly raised her head and spoke now clear and calm. She did not flinch in any way from his wildness but met his eye head on. "Welcome to your home. I am your own wife, Emer, and it's glad I am to rejoice in your victory."

My father did not move for several breaths, as though the words had to burn through a red fog to reach him. Then his eyes seemed to clear a little, and he peered at my mother as if really seeing her.

"Emer." The word was thick with effort.

"Will you bathe, my love? There is clean water prepared for you." Still my mother did not move. I held my breath, knowing this for a critical moment. The cool water would quench the fire that burned in him, if only my father would accept it.

He did not speak but only glowered there, until slowly my mother reached out and took his bloody hand and urged him gently forward to the bath.

CHAPTER 2
HOUND OF THE FORGE

Why had my father come rushing home in such a state? I dared not follow to the baths to find out, but the stables would be safe enough. I slipped out to find Laeg.

My father's charioteer deserves a larger place in the stories, for his horsemanship was a wonder to behold and his faithfulness and courage unshakeable. Yet such is the way of the world: It is the kings and warriors whose praises are sung, not the advisors who guide them nor the charioteers who keep them alive.

He had unyoked the horses, but to my surprise they were not in the stable but out in the paddock, still in their harnesses and war-trappings. The Black had his nose deep in a grain bucket; still I gave him a wide berth as I edged past. He had a vicious leg on him, and I had seen him shatter an unwary groom's knee.

Laeg had tethered The Gray to the apple tree that shaded one end of the paddock and was cleaning out his hooves. I forced myself to walk carefully, not wanting to spill the jar of beer I had thought to take from our stores on my way out. Silently I held it out to him.

His eyebrows, furrowed in concentration, lifted at the sight. Nodding his thanks, he put down the pick and stretched out a long freckled arm for my drink. Everything about Laeg was long—legs, arms, even his narrow face.

"I'll not deny I've a terrible thirst," he said. "My thanks to you, Luaine."

"Laeg, why have you not stabled the horses?" I blurted. I didn't even wait for him to take a swallow.

Laeg drank anyway and then looked down at me for a long moment, his face grave.

"Your father is setting out again, as soon as may be," he said finally. "He has stopped here only to speak with your ma and give instructions to his men."

"But why?" I persisted. "What has happened?"

Laeg shook his head. "That is for your parents to tell you, little one." Then he grinned, but it was not a grin to make you smile back. It scared me. "The Hound is on the hunt," he said, "and his prey will regret the day he caught their scent."

Ξ

The Hound of Ulster, they called him. Hound of the Forge.

My father, born Setanta, earned his warrior's name as a young boy. Cu Culain—the hound of Culain. Culain was a smith, maker of the finest weaponry and armor in all Ulster. His dog, though, was a beast to be dreaded. Huge, savage, heedless of any hand but its master's, it was loosed each night to stand guard and would tear apart any unlucky intruder.

One night my father, just a small boy at the time, followed King Conchobor's chariot tracks to a feast at Culain's home, batting a ball with a hurley stick along the road to amuse himself as he ran. The dog, clamoring in a murderous fury, sprang at him. The men inside rushed out at the commotion, fearing to find someone dead. But my father had batted his hurley ball right down the hound's throat, and then he dashed it to death on a rock, with no injury to himself at all.

Culain, though, was grieved, for the great hound had guarded his home and flocks and herds. So my father, little as he was, promised to keep watch in the dog's place until another could be found and trained. And Cathbad the druid said that Cuchulainn should be my father's name from that day forward.

I had heard Laeg call my father "Cucuc"—little hound. It was a mark of the friendship and trust that was between them. But now when he spoke of the Hound, and flashed his teeth in that wolf's grin, I saw with a chill that it was no hearth-dog Cuchulainn was named for. It's a battle-hound he was, the watchdog of our people.

Ξ

It was not skill at arms, or even the battle-frenzy, that won my father the championship of Ulster. This tale was my favorite as a child, the one I would beg our poet, Lasair, to recount, for it never failed to make my heart beat fast with fear and my eyes grow round with wonder. And I still think on it often—for it reminds me of the manner of man who sired me and of the courage I should find within myself as well. At that time there were three contending for the championship: Laegaire, Conall and my father. And they were set many trials by Conchobor, but although my father always prevailed, the other two would not accept his championship, but made excuses for every contest.

Conchobor could not have his best men at each other's throats, so at last he sent them to Cu Roi of Munster to have the matter judged. But he warned them: "He will give you a right judgment, but it is only a brave man will ask it from him, for he is wise in all sorts of enchantments." So off they went to Munster, only to return with the issue unsettled, for Cu Roi had been away on his own journey.

Well, time passed, and the championship remained unclaimed. Then one night, into the hall lumbers this great fellow, frightful to look at and massive in build. He is clothed in rough undressed skins and in his one hand he bears the biggest ax they have any of them ever seen. He says his name is Uath, the Stranger, and that he has traveled all Ireland looking for only one thing: a man who will keep his word and hold to an agreement.

"What agreement is that?" they ask.

And it's a strange thing indeed. For Uath says he wants someone to strike off his head with the ax, and then on the morrow, he will come and strike off their own head! And, he says, since the men of Ulster have such a name for greatness and strength, surely there is one among them who could hold to such a promise.

Well, who would be in fear of a dead man? Up swaggers Laegaire. "I'm your man," says he, and Uath lays his head on a block and gives Laegaire the ax, and doesn't Laegaire swing it and fill the house with the man's blood right there.

Now, I cannot explain this next part. I, of all people, know that there are many mysteries in the world, that there is magic in the sacred places and in the secret words, but I have never seen a magic like this. Yet all there saw it and believed it too. For Uath rose up all headless, gathered up his head and walked out of that hall. And you can imagine the despair that was upon Laegaire.

The next night, the stranger returned—but Laegaire did not. He hadn't the heart. It is one thing to face death in battle, when the blood boils in your veins and the spear is eager in your hands. Another thing, it is, to lie down like a sheep to slaughter. So Conall stood up, and said he would take the challenge instead, and sliced off Uath's neck with a mighty blow.

And the next night—no Conall. And Uath mocked and sneered at the Ulstermen, and then he asked, "Where is the one they call Cuchulainn, till I see if his word is any better than the others'?" "I will keep my word," said my father and swept off the man's head in a second.

The next night my father knew was his last. "For," he said, "I would rather meet death than break my word."

And when Uath came, my father laid himself down on the block and submitted to his own death.

The stranger swung his blade up until it crashed into the rafters—and then swept it down with a powerful stroke. But the ax-head bit into the floorboards beside Cuchulainn's head and never harmed him at all. For it was Cu Roi, under an enchanted disguise, and this was his test.

"Rise up, Cuchulainn," he said. "The championship of the heroes of Ireland is yours from this day out. For of all the heroes of Ulster, there is not one to compare with you in courage and in bravery and in truth."

No one tried to put himself before my father after that.

CHAPTER 3
THE LONE DEFENDER

What manner of woman, you may be thinking, could hold her own with a man like Cuchulainn? My mother did so, for she had grace and spirit both, and a quick mind, and was never daunted in the least by my father's powers. They had their troubles over the years, to be sure, but I do not believe the love between them was ever broken.

I used to love to hear my mother tell of their courtship. And she never minded repeating the story, at least not its first part.

To hear her tell, my father, a boy too young to even grow a beard, arrived at her home very full of himself indeed: "All in his finery and gold, he was, with his hair such beautiful colors all flowing and his wondrous chariot, puffed up from being the darling of every woman in King Conchobor's court." And she would sniff as she described him, as no doubt she sniffed as he careered up to her where she sat on the lawn with her needlework and her girl companions.

"He spoke in a riddling tongue to me," she said, "and he maintains that was by way of keeping his mission secret from the other maids, but it's only a half-wit could have mistaken his intent. I maintain it was to test my own wits—and fair play to him, for the wife of Cuchulainn should by no means be stupid." He had little to worry about on that score—my mother was daughter to the druid-king Forgall the Wily and had been better schooled than many a noble warrior. She gave him riddles right back and wasted no time in letting him know she was not only quick of tongue but also well-guarded by many great champions against upstarts such as himself.

"Why do you not count me as a strong man as good as those others?" he asked her, and she replied tartly, "Why should I then, when you are still but a boy yourself?" And so, rather than evaluating Emer's worthiness, my father found himself proving his own deeds and training and qualities.

"And then, the cheeky devil"—and my mother always laughed at this part—"he looked right down the top of my dress and announced, 'On that fair plain will I rest my weapon!'"

That, of course, was the beginning of the now-famous feats my mother set down for him to accomplish before he would be allowed to touch her "fair plain"—impossible feats that he accepted with his usual confidence, saying merely, "It is said, it is done."

But my mother's heart was already his before he had completed even the first test, before indeed the end of their conversation, or so I hold. For I saw, as she talked, how this was not her favorite part of the story. Her favorite part came earlier, when she dutifully told Cuchulainn that he should be after wooing her older sister, for Forgall had decreed that the oldest must be the first to wed.

"Truly," he had replied, "it is not with your sister, but with yourself, I have fallen in love." And her face would soften and become faraway as she told it, and her mouth curl with a smile that was not for me.

☰

The part of the story that I learned later is not so pretty. King Forgall set himself against the match, for the Druid's Sight had warned him that Cuchulainn would bring him harm. My father had traveled to Alba to train under the famous warrior woman, Scathach. When he returned to Emer, he found her dwelling-place fortified against him by Forgall and his men. And though Cuchulainn managed to spare Emer's three brothers in the ensuing fight, Forgall fell from the wall and died, and so his prophecy came true, and my mother lost her father in gaining her heart's desire.

But at Emain Macha they had a great welcome from the king and all his company, and my parents were wed at last.

Ξ

I came back from the paddock to find our house, Dun Dealgan, in a turmoil, stirred up like an ants' nest by my father's return. My parents swept through the main room, sending servants scurrying with messages and tasks. I followed in their wake, unnoticed.

"No, Emer, no carts. You must travel fast. Take only what you can load in the chariot."

My mother sighed. "I just hate to think of them tramping through Dun Dealgan, helping themselves to our—"

"Emer." My father reached out and laid his hand over my mother's arm, stopping her as she stuffed clothing and jewelry into a basket. He turned her around to face him, threaded his hands into her hair and leaned in to kiss her. "It is not our goods, nor our cattle, but yourself and Luaine I would keep from their hands."

"Who are they?" I asked.

My parents turned, startled to find me in the doorway of their chamber. My father came over and squatted down in front of me. I eyed him warily. He seemed himself again, though grim and hard.

"Maeve and Ailill of Connaught have invaded Ulster. I caught sight of them on my way home. They have gathered a great army from every province of Ireland, and they are headed through Muirthemne."

"But why? What quarrel do they have with us?" I asked. At that my mother gave a yelp of laughter, but her voice was bitter.

"There is no quarrel, but only greed and pettiness. That a queen would spend the lives of her people for such trumpery!" Shaking her head in disgust, she turned back to her packing, leaving me as bewildered as before.

"It is Queen Maeve who leads this assault," explained my father. "And while she is a wise and powerful ruler"—at this my mother sniffed—"I have met her, and she is," he insisted. "But in this she is in the wrong. For it irks her that she has no match in all her own herds for Ailill's mighty white bull Finnbennach. Indeed there is only one bull in all of Ireland who is his equal, and that bull is in the Cooley Mountains just beyond Muirthemne."

"She is after Donn Cooley?" The great brown bull was famous for his size and power, and it was told that he was sired in the Otherworld and protected by the warlike Morrigu herself.

"She is indeed. And while she is at it, she is taking whatever else lies in her road. And so you and your mother must ride to Emain Macha to warn the king and summon our troops." He dipped his head down a bit to bring our eyes level, and I saw in his a hint of a twinkle. "It is a hero you will be, little dove, for the saving of Ulster," he said. "Will you do it?"

I nodded solemnly, caught up in the drama of the moment. Then the obvious question struck me.

"What about you? Are you not coming?"

The twinkle died. "This is a border outpost, and I am sworn to defend the border. My men and I will make them pay dear for their passage, until the full might of Ulster falls upon them."

I was too young to comprehend the numbers involved, or the danger; it seemed to me my father had a great troop of men, and I could hardly see the need of any more. In truth, he had some three thousand serving under him throughout the region of Muirthemne, most of them farmers and craftsmen under bond. Some of his local men he sent as messengers to summon the warriors in outlying areas. Some he sent to warn the settlements and farms that lay in the army's path; a handful remained at Dun Dealgan to protect our own people. Setting forth with him that day, Cuchulainn had maybe three hundred men.

And Queen Maeve? Her army moved like a cloud of locusts through the land. Eighteen regiments of three thousand, some say, plus the women, druids and bards who traveled with them. And behind them were driven the growing herd of women, children, cattle and sheep they plundered along the way.

≡

The morning haze had gathered itself into islands of fleecy cloud by the time we set off, my mother prancing on her fiery little mare, myself wedged into the chariot amongst baskets and chests and weaponry. Besides us two, there were only the chariot driver and Berach, the arms master, riding guard on his big-boned roan. His ugly face was eager, and I knew his thoughts flew ahead to my father's promise that he should return with the Ulstermen to do battle.

Cuchulainn strode out to see us off. He had put on his war-harness—the stiff hide breastplate and wide belt to repel spear and sword thrusts—so that he looked to have just hacked himself free of some great beast that still clutched at him. My mother leaned far over her saddle to embrace him. "Ride fast and be wary, Emer," he said. "There may be scouts far ahead of the main troops."

My mother straightened and turned her horse around. "Be wary, yourself," she said briskly. "The might of Ulster will soon be at your side."

But my father motioned her to wait, and came to the chariot and pulled me to my feet. From within the stiff crust of armor that enclosed him, he pulled a richly tooled leather scabbard and slowly drew from it a sword, exquisite but slim—made for a woman's hand. "This is for you." My eyes widened at the sheen of the blade, the green gems studded into the hand guard, the smooth bronze grip. I reached for it—and he drew it away.

"It is not yet yours to keep, mind. It will take a few years' growth and training before you can be mistress of such a weapon. But it does not do to travel unarmed in wartime." He threaded the strap around my waist and cinched it tight. "If you have need of it, you will know how to wield it." And though the sword, in truth, was too long for my small frame, I felt the pride and courage swell up in me at the thought of carrying such a fine thing.

And then we were off, and my dreams of glory were swept away in the need to keep from careening right out of the jolting chariot. Chariots are built for speed and maneuverability, not comfort, with only two iron-rimmed wheels and bare room for two standing men and their weapons and gear. I clutched at the side-rails and wished I were big enough to ride free like my mother. She floated ahead at an easy canter, the red flanks of her horse and the bronze of her hair both lighting up like beacons when a shaft of sunlight found them.

CHAPTER 4
THE WEAKNESS OF ULSTER

I will never forget my first sight of Emain Macha, King Conchobor's great hill fort. Our shadows slanted long behind us, though the spring sun would not set for some hours. It had been a long afternoon's ride, the broad way that led us across Muirthemne's open skies shrinking to a narrow track threading its way through the forested hill-country. The boggy stretches where the road was reinforced with planking were the worst—I thought the drumming of the chariot wheels would rattle the teeth out of my very head. Then the trees gave way once more to cleared land and the hills smoothed out to gentle swells. At last my mother pointed out a bump on the horizon, and I watched it grow before us into a looming mound, walled and studded with buildings. Once their destination was plain the horses' pace quickened, so that at the end we came pounding up the hill to the gate with such a flourish that there was quite a crowd gathered to meet us.

I had longed to visit Emain Macha ever since I first heard my parents' tales of Conchobor's court. The huge Royal House of red yew, the troupe of boys training at games and warriors' arts on the great playing field, the poets and bards, the valiant champions of the Red Branch…and of course the feasts. I could not wait to be old enough to attend a grand feast.

Mind you, those feasts could be very rough. There were all kinds of contests, challenges and jockeying for position, which with men quick to anger and full of ale could quickly lead to an out-and-out fight. There was a poet there at the time, one Bricriu, who took perverse delight in stirring up trouble. My father said Bricriu once told three different wives, each on their way to join the men in the feasting hall, that if they arrived first they would be set above all the other women of Ulster. And so they began running, my mother and two others, each with all their women, and my father said the noise of them approaching made the very ground shake. "We thought it was the enemy rushing toward us," he said, "but when Sencha realized that Bricriu had set the women to quarreling, that terrified him more than any foe. 'Shut the door of the hall against them,' he yelled, 'or those that are dead among us will be more than those that are living!' And with that the doorkeepers shut the doors." How it made me giggle when he told it, to picture all the great heroes of Ulster locked in their feasting hall, afraid of their own women!

"Emer was there first," my father told me, grinning with pride, "but the door was barred. So they bade the women to have a war of words to prove who was best, but Laegaire and Conall did not like the outcome, for Emer was like a very poet singing the praises of herself and myself."

"Oh, I laid it on," my mother agreed, "the insults as well." And they laughed, remembering how my mother had boasted with such eloquence of her own beauty and virtue, while likening the other women to plain cows. Their happiness with each other was like a warm cloak tucked around me, and I thought to myself that my own two parents must be peerless in all of Ireland.

So despite my rough ride, I was nearly beside myself with excitement as we came to a stop outside the high fence that surrounded the king's dun. My mother was recognized and admitted right away and rode straight to the Royal House. It sprawled over the settlement, dwarfing every other building in the compound. How does it stay up? I wondered, marveling at the immensity of it. The cone of the roof soared so high into the sky I had to crane my head as far back as it would go to see the tip. A wonder it doesn't catch fire when the sun's overhead, I thought. While I goggled, my mother dismounted neatly, passed the reins to Berach and lifted me from the chariot. A quick gesture smoothed her hair and skirt, and then she turned to address the door-guards.

"I come from Cuchulainn, Champion of Ulster. I must speak with the king immediately."

They exchanged looks.

"He is not here at present, Lady Emer."

"Sencha, then. Is he here?"

They shook their heads in unison, but seemed hesitant to say more. My mother's eyes flashed, and I thought to myself that the king's men would soon wish they had been more helpful. Her voice, when she spoke, was a cold whip.

"Ulster is under attack. While we stand here exchanging pleasantries, Maeve of Connaught marauds through our countryside unhindered. Now who in the name of the gods has authority in Emain Macha?"

The men straightened in shock. "Your pardon, Lady Emer, we thought it was...well, we knew your husband was not well-pleased to have been overlooked for Celthair's feast."

My ears pricked up. I had been aware that something had angered my father when he last was home—he had ridden off, in fact, in an abrupt fury—but I had not known the cause.

"No, he was not well-pleased," my mother agreed. "And well it is that he restrained himself from vengeance on his friends, and sought a more fitting foe instead, for it is because of his patrols that the armies of Connaught have been discovered. And now, you will answer my question, before the whole of the province is overrun!"

"They are still at the feast—Conchobor and all his nobles." It was the older of the two guards who spoke, a man with a grizzle of gray in his hair and beard. "They left four days ago and have not yet returned."

"They will return now." My mother could have been the queen of Ulster herself, so assured was her authority. "We have traveled the afternoon without rest or food. You will bring us provisions now, such as may be eaten on the move, and a guide. I will go myself to rouse them."

Ξ

Cathbad, the king's chief druid, was there. He had returned alone from the feast early the previous day, his old bones craving a proper bed and his mind uneasy. When he heard Emer's report, though, he declared he himself would accompany my mother to Dun Lethglaise, Celthair's house on the shores of the River Quoile. A sudden fear came over me: that I would be left behind in the care of some strange woman of Conchobor's household. I felt battered and tired from the long chariot ride, but I would travel to the ends of Ireland, I thought, rather than leave my mother now.

I needn't have worried—at least not about that. The chariot was to be left behind, but not me. To my horror, the fellow who brought Cathbad's horse scooped me up under the arms and planted me in front of Cathbad himself. That frightened me more than all the warriors of Connaught! His long gray beard blew in the wind and tickled my neck, and his breath whistled over my head, but I didn't dare move a muscle. I held myself stiff and tried to become an invisible weightless thing. But the horse's gait was smooth and soothing, and after we had eaten, the fluttery feeling in my stomach quieted. I remember my mother passing me a cloak against the cool of the evening as the sun sank. The sky blazed with fiery color, dazzling against the dark hills.

I woke with a start as the motion stopped, first confused at where I was, and then appalled to find myself slumped against the chief druid of Ulster. I jerked away in alarm, stammering an apology, and then another as I overbalanced and nearly fell from the horse.

"It's all right, Luaine." His voice was a soft murmur, spoken only to me. "It's not eating children I am here for." It was a tired joke, even to a seven-year-old, but it reassured me all the same.

"Well, then," he said, and I could hear the grimace in his voice as he stretched out his back. "Let us go in, and see why there is no one here to greet us."

≡

The men were in no condition to greet us. The smell that billowed out as Berach pulled open the oak doors was terrible—vomit, urine, and gods above! that was only the start of it. I recoiled, retching, and ran back to stand with the horses.

But my mother held her ground. She cast her eyes around the dark interior, found a wall bracket and pulled out the torch. "Do you have a flint, Berach?" Then, holding the light high, she led the two men into the fetid hall. I heard groans, and calls for help, and horrible, racking retching noises that made my own belly flip over in disgust.

The story that eventually emerged was this: The feasting and drinking had gone on for three days and three nights, by which time the food had given out. Near dawn on the third night, three men had staggered into the adjoining storehouse demanding food, and when the cook had insisted there was no more, they had beaten the poor man nearly senseless before he was able to escape their drunken fists and run from the building. Finally, roaming the grounds, they had found a haunch of beef at the top of the midden heap. It had gone off and been thrown out, but they dragged it back to the fire, cut off the obviously green parts and roasted the rest. The next morning they woke their fellows with a triumphant breakfast, and by noon the whole lot of them were desperately ill.

I do not know if Celthair was ever able to live in that house again. The men suffered such ague and griping cramps that many were unable even to stagger outside to relieve themselves. They were sick and needed nursing, but in all honesty, they were so repellent in their drunkenness and wallowing filth, that the most dedicated healer would have been hard-pressed to go near them. Certainly the servants had not been up to the task. They had fled, risking their master's wrath rather than face such a horror.

My mother emerged from the building in angry despair. "They are useless!" she railed. "Not one man in all of Ulster fit to lead an army to battle! And where is the pride and might of our people now?"

≡

Safe behind the red mare's flank, I watched the drama unfold. Berach and Cathbad had built up a fire on the riverbank, and then, with makeshift torches, they plunged back into the house.

They had returned again with a man slung between them, his feet dragging weakly behind. My mother was grim, her lips pressed together so tight they all but disappeared as she flung off her cloak and rolled back her sleeves. She stripped the filthy clothes off the man, and it was only as I heard Cathbad coaxing him into the dark water that I realized who it was.

It was the white backside of the king I was staring at, and it made me sick with shame to see him like that, streaked with his own filth and weak as a newborn calf. The river must have been ice-cold so early in the year, but they all four waded through the reeds into the dark water, and my mother herself scrubbed him down while the two men supported him. She must have rinsed out his clothes too, for I heard the wet slap of them as she threw them onto the shore. "Useless," she said again, and I wasn't sure if she meant the king or her attempt at washing his clothing. Conchobor was brought naked and shivering to the fire, where he was wrapped in Berach's cloak, and at last my mother made her way back to me. By then I had let my legs fold under me and was curled up in my own cloak in the dewy grass, struggling to keep my eyes open.

"Let's go find the stables, dove," she said, and I pulled myself to my feet. Her skirt dripped and clung to her legs as we led the three horses. The outbuildings were no more than black shadows rising against the stars, but the paths were smooth and we found the right one without much trouble. The stable, at least, was clean and orderly, shoveled out that afternoon by the looks of it. I breathed deep, grateful for the familiar smells: horse and fresh straw, leather and the sharp bite of urine. There was a pallet in the tack corner with a small oil lamp on a shelf beside it. My mother lit the lamp from her torch, heaped the pallet with fresh straw, spread out her cloak and announced, "Bedtime."

I was in no mood to protest. She covered me with my own cloak, and then she knelt down and kissed my cheek. "I'll come back to see to the horses and then join you when I can. You'll be all right here, Luaine? Not frightened?"

I shook my head and nuzzled into my mother's cloak. This felt safe, like home. Much, much better than being out there with… "Is the king dying, Ma?"

She gazed at me, her eyes dark in the lamplight, as if considering whether to answer. The light caught her hair as she shook her head. "Cathbad doesn't think so. He is searching now for ingredients to make a medicine." Again her lips pressed against each other as if to hold back the rest of what she wished to say.

"Sleep well, then, little one." My mother turned to a rack hung with horse blankets and stacked her arms high before disappearing into the dark.

Horse blankets for a king, I thought with a guilty giggle. I fell asleep listening to the whispery rustle of rats in the grain bags.

Ξ

The slow deep rumble had woven through my dreams, so that I woke to a voice I already knew. I didn't know its owner, though, and I stayed very quiet and small in my bed while I listened. My mother was gone—she had squeezed in beside me in the night, but her place was cold now.

Slowly the sound of his work came closer. I listened to the scrape of the shovel, the rustle of forked straw, the dry sibilance of grain buckets filling—the sure, deliberate movements and quiet talk of a man who knows how to put animals at ease. By the time he came to my mother's red mare, I had already decided I liked him. I confess I still hold the childish belief that men who are good with animals are trustworthy with people as well.

"Ah, now." The footfalls stopped. "Aren't you a beauty, then?" he breathed, and a swell of pride warmed me. He murmured to her as he cleaned her stall, admiring her. "Used to stabling with the best too, aren't you? The great horses of Cuchulainn himself."

"She is prettier than those two," I called out. Ceara was my favorite, and I didn't see why she should always stand in the shadow of The Gray and The Black.

There was a pause, and then a surprised chuckle. The slow footsteps came to the half-wall that divided my little room from the main barn, and I sat up hurriedly.

"Awake then, Mistress Luaine?" He swept off his cap and bowed: a small, dark man with a jumble of teeth and a ready smile. "I am Seanan, at your service," he said.

"Where is my mother?"

"At work already, laboring to put the men of Ulster on their feet." He shook his head. "A right wonder she is, your mother." That seemed cheeky, and I frowned, not quite up to the task of reprimanding a grown man. He paid me no mind, but continued. "She hoped to return before you awoke, but if not, asked me to look out for you. Are you hungry?"

Gods, yes. The hunger awoke in me as soon as it was spoken, and on its heels, more urgent still, the need to urinate.

"There's a trench out back where you can take a—" Seanan stopped short and waved a hand vaguely at the doorway. No doubt it had occurred to him that "piss" might not be a proper word for a young noble lady.

Ξ

We were two nights at Celthair's dun, nursing Conchobor and waiting for him to be fit to travel. On the second day, the house servants, or most of them, returned. Word had got out that my mother had taken charge and with someone to direct them, they regained their courage. She wasted no time chastising them but put them straight to work: restocking the cookhouse (which thankfully was a separate building adjoining the main house), finding fresh clothing for the king, fetching Cathbad the herbs he needed. One asked whether they shouldn't also fetch out and tend their master. At that my mother's sniff reached new heights of expressiveness.

"It is all one to me," she said at last. "He is your master, so no doubt you owe him your service. For myself, I should think a man who manages to poison his guests ought at least to suffer alongside them."

The servants exchanged uneasy looks, not knowing whether they had been given leave or not, but at length Celthair was brought forth and washed up and dosed with Cathbad's brew. But my mother never paid him any mind at all, except to tell him in parting that it was only due to the loyalty of his servants that he was so well tended. Thanks to her, he never knew that they had abandoned him in his illness, but instead was grateful for their care.

Ξ

We left under a threatening sky. The river was black and choppy, uneasy under the ridges of cloud—a row of dark underbellies swollen with rain—that pressed over us. My mother eyed the clouds, then the little canopy Berach was fixing over the cart Conchobor would travel in, and sighed. "Let's hope the man doesn't drown before he recovers," she muttered in his ear. Berach snorted his agreement. "He will arrive alive, Lady Emer, if I have to bail all the way to Emain," he promised, and I saw my mother's impatient anxiety reflected in his own pale eyes.

CHAPTER 5
ULSTER RISES

It's strange, isn't it, how a thing can be good and bad at the same time? Our stay at Emain Macha was like that.

The place itself was so different from what I expected, I couldn't help but be disappointed. Not that my parents had exaggerated— it was all there, just as they had described: the boys' long playing field, the Speckled House full of war trophies and weapons, and of course Conchobor's great house itself. My mother and I stayed there, in the large richly furnished room that was always kept free for Cuchulainn and Emer. I walked right around the outside of the Royal House one morning, numbering one finger for every step, trying to see how many times over I would count all my fingers before I closed the circle. I forget now how many it was—enough for me to realize that our own home of Dun Dealgan was like a farmer's cottage compared to the king's house. It took five circles of huge posts inside the walls to support the weight of the roof! And while we had a partial second story—a ring of small storage areas tucked under the eaves—the Royal House at Emain Macha had a full ceiling, with as much space above as below. And beautiful! Everywhere I looked there was carving and tapestry, the shine of beaten bronze and copper, rich fabrics and polished wood.

What was missing were the champions. The feasts and feats, the singing and storytelling. There was only the bustle of servants

tending to King Conchobor, and long worried faces, and Cathbad
sweeping around giving orders, and my mother…

My mother was driven by an invisible lash, night and day.
She seemed never to rest, even when she was still—and she was
so rarely still. I cannot say she neglected me, yet I could tell she
did not *see* me. Her eyes were faraway, with my father. Cathbad
worked as hard as she did, and without him perhaps all her efforts
would have been in vain. He took a handful of his apprentices to
the kitchens and set them to brewing huge batches of medicines,
while my mother hovered at the king's bedside, urging him when-
ever he seemed at all lucid to send messengers to all his chieftains'
men, summoning them to assemble for battle. But I heard her tell
Cathbad afterward, almost beside herself with frustration, that
he seemed unable to follow the thread of her account.

"He roused himself once and told me to summon Cuchulainn,
for the love of all that's holy!" And she gave a harsh caw of a laugh
that brought the tears to my eyes and made my heart twist.

The next day, Cathbad sent two of his druids and all the
apprentices—not the noble children he tutored in history and lore
but some twenty destined for the druid's feathered cape—back
to Celthair's dun. They led wagons filled with jugs and padded
with blankets, and others piled with their own provisions, and
each was instructed to take one man away from the squalor of
the house and tend to him. I learned later that one of Cathbad's
medicines was nothing but a tea of slippery elm and raspberry
leaf, a simple remedy that any country housewife might brew
up for a child with the squiddles. The other, though, a chalky
sludge with the rank smell of marsh-mud—that was a mystery.
All I knew was that it had taken the combined might of Cathbad

and Berach both to force a half-cup of the foul mixture into King Conchobor when he hardly had strength to lift his head.

I had watched them load up the wagons that morning, careful to keep out of the way but still edging as close as I could. I was lonely, wanting my own home and my mother as she used to be, and then feeling guilty for such selfishness. It was comforting to be near these serious young men and their orderly preparations. Strangely enough, it was even comforting to be near Cathbad—my fear of him must have floated away on the shores of the River Quoile. He caught my eye once and nodded at me gravely as if I were a grown-up. I can't find the words to describe how that made me feel, but I remember it made me sit up straighter and lift my chin, wanting to be the person he had greeted.

We watched the wagons rumble down the road, and then Cathbad turned to me. "How are you faring, Luaine, in all this turmoil?"

"Fine, sir," I answered, but then I looked quickly at the ground, afraid his Druid's Sight would recognize my lie.

He let me wriggle in it a while, and then he said, "The men of Ulster will rise, Luaine, and ride to Cuchulainn's side, and when that is done your mother will come back to you."

I nodded, still examining my feet, but his gnarled finger dipped under my chin and brought my eyes up to his. They were black and penetrating, impossible to escape, but I found I did not wish to. Those dark eyes bored into me; then he nodded slowly at whatever he read there. "A lonely long wait all the same for you, isn't it?" And not waiting for my reply, he asked, "Tell me, do you like animals?"

I had barely drawn breath to answer when he forestalled me

with a smile. "I thought so. Well then, I have a friend for you. A little company for your stay here."

Ξ

If Cathbad had done nothing more for me—and he has done much—I would be in his debt still for this one thing. Little enough has come with me from my old life, but Fintan perches on my shoulder still.

I laughed when I learned his name.

"Fintan? It's a lovely name, but for a raven?" *White fire*, for a bird as black as pitch. "Is it a riddle?"

"In a way." Cathbad's old eyes crinkled in amusement. "A secret, rather." He smoothed down the glossy feathers, scratched the shaggy ruff under the bird's heavy bill and spread out its left wing. I saw it then: a single white feather, a secondary that lay hidden behind its neighbors until the full stretch exposed it to view. Striking, the way each color seemed to intensify from the contrast against the other, the black dense and bottomless, the white leaping out against it brighter than snow or sea foam or the white gulls themselves. It drew my eyes and swelled in my vision until I could see nothing else.

"Come on, then. Come and meet him."

I started and looked up to find Cathbad studying me. He nodded once, as if in answer to a question I had not asked. "He is no ordinary raven, but you need not fear him. Indeed I believe you will get on very well together."

His plumage was soft and glossy, yet bristly stiff if you ruffled it the wrong way. Fintan allowed me to stroke him a few times, and then he tilted his head and fixed me with one brilliant black eye. He became agitated, clacking his beak and tossing his head up and down like a nervous horse, so that I stepped back, alarmed, and asked Cathbad what was wrong. He just smiled and told me to be still.

Suddenly, with a great flurry of flapping wings, Fintan launched himself from Cathbad's arm and landed on my shoulder. I staggered a little from the sudden weight—a full-grown raven is no small burden—and gasped at the hard clutch of his talons. But I held my ground, and as he sidestepped over to press against my ear I felt I might burst from the delight of it.

With an ear-splitting squawk, Fintan lifted his tail and let loose a white stream down my tunic. Cathbad laughed. "A sure sign that he likes you."

≡

The door banged open, and in the time it took Cathbad to whirl about, the kindly old man vanished. The very air about him crackled with cold outrage, and I saw that I had not been wrong to fear him. He was chief druid, and not even the king himself could barge headlong into his house without asking leave.

Apparently my mother could. She stood wild-eyed in the doorway, and Cathbad's rage evaporated.

"What is it, Emer?"

Something terrible, that I knew. For days she had been wound like a spring, hounded with an overriding purpose. Now she looked beaten, sick with some grief that bled away her strength.

"The boys have gone."

I did not know an old one could move so fast. His angry curse rang still in my ears, but Cathbad was already striding across the compound, pulling my mother along by the elbow.

Fintan and I were forgotten, but we could piece together well enough what had happened. The youth of Emain Macha, spurred on by my mother's urgency or their own dreams of glory, had left their games and taken up arms, riding to join my father's stand against Connaught.

I pictured them sneaking off at dawn, high-spirited and eager to prove themselves, and I wanted desperately to believe it would be as they imagined. But my mother's face had told another tale, and so did the black fist that clutched my heart. No troop of boys, however courageous and full of promise, could match an army of seasoned soldiers.

"They will none of them return," I whispered, and Fintan sat silent on my thin shoulder as I hid my face in my hands and cried for them all.

Ξ

The boys were beyond recall, but their departure spurred Cathbad into decisive action. He sent out the summons himself, in the king's own name. It made only a day's difference, for by the next morning the king was lucid, able to order in the troops himself. That one day did not save the boys, but it may have saved my father.

Emer was giddy with relief as she told me. "Oh, the king was well enough to be red with indignation when he heard what Cathbad had done. But he soon saw the sense of it, and there is no doubt he is on the mend. I spooned the gruel into him myself, and it has all stayed where it belongs." And then, as she had not done since we left Dun Dealgan, she scooped me up in her arms and swung me around in an extravagant hug. "It won't be long now, dove."

Nor was it. Only that afternoon men started trickling in from Celthair's dun, pale and bandy-legged but determined. By the time they were fit to fight, their forces were camped all around Emain Macha. No longer would my father stand alone.

CHAPTER 6
THE QUEEN OF SORROW

On the night before Ulster's forces rode to war, Conchobor held a feast for his champions. And though I had tried hard to be obedient and uncomplaining on this journey, now that my mother's burden was lessened it is shameless I was in begging to attend.

"Please, Ma!" I was losing hope but couldn't give it up. I clutched at her hand, dragging against her brisk stride, and promised earnestly, "I'll be no trouble. I won't say a word. And I'll go straight to bed after!"

Shucking me off with an impatient flick, my mother opened her mouth for the last denial I would get without a slap to help it sink in—and shut it again. She looked down at me, eager and jittery as a hound before it is loosed, and dimpled into a smile.

"Why not then, after all? You've been no trouble at all so far, with little enough attention from me. And Lugh knows, there will be no carousing into the wee hours this time."

I was a little disappointed by that. "Why won't there be?"

"Conchobor will need men with clear heads in the morning. Besides, there is too much to do."

That I could believe. Emain Macha had buzzed like a bee-hive all day with the preparations. I could hear it buzzing still, through the little slit of a window that was fashioned into the outer wall of our room: shouted instructions, hurried footfalls, the sibilance of blades on the whetstone, hammering from the smithies and the rumble of carts. There was no one sat idle that day.

Ξ

I did not see her at first, so full were my eyes with everything else. Rows of bright banners hung from the ceiling rafters, which ran right across the vast hall to support the floor of the rooms above. Torches and candles fluttered with every movement, and my eyes were dazzled by the gold and copper and bright swatches of color on the guests.

My mother's seat on the women's side was near the king's table, for Emer was first among Ulster's women, as my father was first among the champions. The women's side was not so crowded as the men's, for not all the warriors' wives had made the journey to Emain. My mother bent her head to me and pointed out the heroes I had heard my father speak of: Sencha, the spokesman and peacemaker of the men of Ulster; Conchobor's sons Cuscraid and Finnchad; Laegaire and Conall Cearnach, both warriors of renown. I craned my neck, marking each, and asked, "Where is Fergus?"

My father had often spoken highly of Fergus, one of the men who had fostered him when he came to Emain Macha as a boy. So I was surprised to see my mother's face harden.

"Do not speak of him here!" she cautioned, hissing the words between her teeth close in my ear. I nodded, bewildered, and fell silent.

My eyes must have drifted over the woman sitting at the king's left hand several times before actually taking notice. So still and plainly dressed she was, that she seemed to blend into the wood of the walls. It was as if a pocket of mist surrounded her, a mist that dimmed the clash of color in the hall and muted the laughter and boasting as it drifted past her.

She is alone among all these people, I thought, and it was the first time I understood that this could be so.

But once my eye found her, all I could look at was the young woman at the king's side. Her head was bent, so I could see only a white brow and the river of her hair, pale and smooth as corn silk, shining in the torchlight. Her pale arms were thin—too thin—but she made no move to eat. Indeed she made no move at all, but merely sat there, her eyes glued to the hands that rested in her lap.

"Ma." I tugged at her sleeve, a little afraid to ask. When she had swallowed her meat and bent her ear to me, I whispered my question. "Who is the lady beside the king?"

My mother sighed, and I could tell she regretted bringing me. There were too many expressions on her face to sort out. I thought I could read pity, but she seemed angry too. I had to strain to hear her reply through the din:

"That is the king's young queen, Deirdriu. I had not thought she would be here."

All through the long meal my eyes kept returning to the silent woman. Just once I saw her raise her head—when a table overturned at the back of the hall, and the crash and clatter of it startled her from her reverie.

I caught my breath at the sight of her face. The beauty of it was a bright star in a black sky. Her eyes scanned the hall, and I saw the pain undisguised in them and the purple smudges underneath, but still she shone. I wondered if she was a woman of the Sidhe, a visitor from the enchanted land that lies below and beyond our own. The thought came to me unbidden: she is lovelier than my mother. Immediately I tried to take it back, but I couldn't. My mother's beauty glowed with life and strength, like the sun on a summer's day. But Deirdriu had the fragile unearthly delicacy of the first blush of dawn or the first snowdrop of spring.

She dropped her head and the star winked out. But I could not forget what I had seen nor stop wondering what burden had left its dark mark on her eyes.

Ξ

We rose at dawn to see the men off, and for the first time I understood what an army was. Men and horses, chariots and wagons, more than I had ever imagined, tossed and churned like a vast sea. An ocean of men, I thought, and indeed they did seem to float on the thick morning mist that steamed from the earth and hid the turf in a silvery drifting cloud. When the men clashed their weapons against their shields and shouted for Conchobor, the din seemed to shake the earth as well as the air, throbbing up through my legs and deafening my ears. On his word they thundered south across the plain, all in their companies, and it was not until the last tiny speck had vanished over the last hazy hill that my mother pulled her gaze back from the horizon. She smiled at me and squeezed my hand, but I could tell it was hard for her to turn away and walk back to the walls of Emain. Her heart had ridden out with Ulster's champions to the Cooley Hills, and it was only I who kept her body from following.

Ξ

"They call her Deirdriu of the Sorrows."

On the slow walk back to the gates, Emer consented to speak of the queen.

"I would rather you had not known of her. But if we are to stay in Emain, doubtless you will hear talk." We walked in silence for some time. I suppose my mother was searching for a way to tell the story that would not upset a young girl, but it couldn't be done. And yet I knew if I waited long enough, she would continue, and so she did.

"There was a prophecy about Deirdriu, before she left her mother's belly, that she would be beautiful beyond all others, and that she would bring death and jealous discord to Ulster," my mother said. "So Conchobor, thinking perhaps to forestall any fighting over her, had her raised in an isolated place, out of sight of all men, to be his bride when she grew to womanhood. And in due time, she was brought to the king to be wed, barely out of her girlhood and innocent of the world."

My mother sighed. "And then the prophecy came true."

As soon as he laid eyes upon Deirdriu, the king was desperate with desire. But Deirdriu's eyes, which had never seen a man her own age, rested upon the lovely face and limbs of the young warrior Naoise. She loved him deeply, and he her, and so they fled Emain Macha together, sailing finally to the shores of Alba where they lived together for some years.

Conchobor's men bitterly resented the banishment of Naoise and his two brothers, who had gone with him, for they all three were loved and admired by all of Ulster. But Conchobor burned for Deirdriu. And so he sent Fergus as a messenger to Naoise, saying that he was forgiven and that he and his brothers—and

Deirdriu too, of course—were welcome back in Ulster. And Fergus, unaware of the king's treachery, gave his bond for their safety.

Perhaps you have guessed how this story ends. I did, but then I had Deirdriu's pale, still face to help me. Conchobor set his men upon Naoise and his brothers and killed them, and the king took Deirdriu to his marriage bed. And that is why Fergus was not among the men of Ulster. Outraged at the king's betrayal of his honor, he had left Emain Macha and ridden to Connaught, where he offered his service to Maeve and Ailill.

"But Deirdriu will give the king no pleasure," concluded my mother. "She will not eat with him, or speak with him, or smile in his presence, or even look upon him. Her heart is with Naoise, you see, whatever the king wills."

I pondered this in puzzled silence. I had been raised to revere the king. He was my father's uncle, who had protected and favored him since his boyhood. Cuchulainn was loyal to Conchobor, that I knew—but here was my mother, trying to guard her words but without a doubt blaming Conchobor for Naoise's death.

A terrible thought came to me.

"Ma, was—" I swallowed. "Was my father one of the men?" She knew which men I meant.

"Your father would have no part of it," she replied. She knelt before me in the wet grass and held my shoulders, her green eyes steady on mine. "He would not raise his hand in treachery against his own comrades, not even for a King," she said. "Remember that."

Ξ

I spoke with Deirdriu once. It's a memory that haunts me to this day. Strange, isn't it, that a quiet talk in an orchard would upset me more than what I saw later, but it did.

Cathbad had charged me with Fintan's care while he was off with the armies and, most especially, for taking him out of his dark roundhouse into the light and air every day.

"What if he should fly off and not return?" I asked anxiously.

Cathbad was unconcerned. "If he flies off, it is for his own reasons, Luaine. Fintan stays or goes as he wishes. If I return and find him starved, though, that will be on your head!"

So I learned to crook out my elbow and offer my arm to the big bird, and he never refused but hopped up to my shoulder and dug in his strong toes. And because of Fin, I gained a little extra freedom.

I had been told to stay always within the embankments of Emain Macha. They were big enough for a little girl—it was a good long walk all around the walls, with more people and buildings inside than I had ever seen. But at Dun Dealgan we had looked out over a plain that sloped away from sight like a rolling green ocean, while on the other side the sea itself swept in and out of our bay in its ceaseless tides, and yellow gorse lit up the flanks of the Cooley Hills. Inside Emain it was all buildings and dirt paths; even the playing field's turf was gouged brown and muddy from the boys' games. It all pressed on me somehow.

When my mother first saw me with Fintan on my shoulder, her nose wrinkled in distaste. "Luaine, where did you find that dirty creature? It looks like the old crone of death herself looming over you." When she heard it was Cathbad's bird, though, her eyes went wide.

"He gave you his raven?" She eased herself slowly onto a bench, considering me as I stood puffed with pride, ignoring the pinch of Fin's talons.

"Luaine." I could see she chose her words deliberately. "A druid's raven is very…valuable, and it is not for everyone to even touch it. You must take very good care to follow Cathbad's instructions."

I had my opening.

"Ma, I am to take him out for exercise every day, but I think he would rather be in the trees. Could I not go a little ways into the orchards by the north wall?"

The orchards of Emain—acres and acres of them—drifted right up to the embankment on the northeast side, a quiet glory of white and pink bloom.

Getting to them was harder than I had expected. Rather than take the long way round from the south gate, I had planned to just climb over the wall. I had done it often enough at home.

Here, though, the ditch was on the inside of the wall instead of the outside—which was strange, for how would it hamper an attacking enemy that way? It certainly hampered me, for I had to scramble down, pick my way across the mucky bottom and climb all the way up the other side—the height of the ditch plus the earthen bank, that was—before I even got to the wall. It was a hard climb, and I was glad of the broad walkway at the top of the embankment where I could rest a moment. I eyed the heavy posts of the wall, looking for the best climbing spot, while Fintan poked his beak into likely crannies where beetles or field mice might hide.

The wall itself was not so difficult, but what I saw when I

hoisted my head over the top was daunting: a steep drop down, with no ledge to land on at the foot of the stakes. The fence had been built right at the outside edge of the earthworks, three times a man's height from the top to the ground. I would have to walk back to the gate, after all.

"Does your mother know you are after jumping the wall?"

A girl's voice it was, so I was not scared, though I gave a guilty start all the same. As I squinted into the trees, a willowy figure emerged from the orchard.

"Well?"

I nodded. Even the way she walked was beautiful, I thought. I could look at nothing but her.

"You are sure?" She was so close now I could see the deep, deep blue of her eyes—almost violet, they were—and the dark fringe of lashes so startling against the pale gold of her hair. She seemed amused, and I was glad to have given her even this whisper of happiness.

I smiled and found my voice. "Yes, Lady Deirdriu. I have leave to come to the orchard to exercise my friend Fintan, here."

Deirdriu soon solved my problem. She bade me walk along the embankment until I was directly behind the smokehouse, and when I peeked over the wall, there she was on the far side, tucking up her skirts and climbing—surprisingly quickly—up the embankment. In a moment I had another surprise: a little door in the fence, cut into the posts and so well matched I hadn't even marked it, popped open, and Deirdriu's face peeked through.

"You're just the right size for this," she said. "The guards have to crawl through on their knees." There were pieces of chain staked into the hill to make handholds, and Deirdriu guided me so I was able to slither from one to the next. Soon we were sitting under clouds of pear blossom.

For a long time she was quiet, and so was I. The busy noise of the settlement faded away, replaced by a lazy murmur of bees overhead. Shafts of sunlight poked here and there among the branches, turning the gray bark gold and revealing a thousand dancing motes of dust and pollen in their path. Like a dream-world, I thought, or a held breath, so quiet it was. I watched as Deirdriu gathered little heaps of white petals into her hand and let them flutter through open fingers onto the dark cloth of her skirt.

"Lovely, aren't they?"

I nodded. Her eyes were faraway, and I did not want to bring her back by speaking. One finger stroked the single velvet petal remaining in the palm of her hand.

"I wish I could have covered him with these petals. He was like that, you know, so lovely—gold and green, like the spring. It was he showed me the little door, when we first loved each other. We used to meet in this orchard." Now the brilliant eyes rested on me, bruised violets in the dew. I thought I would weep at the sight of them, but I could not look away.

Her voice was low and sad and private. "I begged him not to come back here. Did I not dream how it would end? Three birds I saw, bearing drops of honey in their mouths, sweet as Conchobor's honeyed lies. But it was drops of blood the birds bore away with them. And now my Naoise is gone, and I am alone with my tears."

"I'm sorry for your grief," I whispered. I had never said those words to anyone before, never tasted the ash of them in my mouth. Deirdriu seemed to really see me then, see how young I was.

"It's sorry I am, little one," she said. "I should not burden you with such talk."

She had, though. It's true that young as I was, I could already draw peoples' stories from them, just by listening and waiting. But there was a strange recklessness to Deirdriu also, despite her quiet manner. She did not hide her heart, not even from a child, and her grief touched me like cold fingers in my belly. They scrabbled and stretched, and I knew suddenly that there was more, and worse, to come.

I scrambled to my feet under pretext of looking for Fintan, trying to thrust aside the bad, scared feeling that was growing in me. I know that feeling now, and it no longer frightens me, but I will never welcome it.

Whistling, searching the trees, I called for Fin. Please don't have flown off, I thought. I need you. I thought of him, I suppose, as a kitten you could cuddle for comfort after scraping your knee. That's another thing I know now: Fintan is no kitten.

He burst out of the leaves in an untidy flapping jumble, landing on a branch behind and above Deirdriu's head. Making me see, he was.

She was backlit in the afternoon sun, her hair a golden halo around her. But her face—it was all darkness, a fractured black emptiness. The cold fingers clenched, and I saw blood spatter in the darkness, and I heard my own stricken cry.

"Lady! What is it that cloaks you in blackness?"

Her voice, floating out of the shadow, was calm and dreamy. "Conchobor says he will give me to the man who killed my Naoise if he does not get my welcome on his return. But Eoghan will never lie with me. This I have sworn."

I turned tail and ran, ran from the black clutch of the icy fingers and the desolation that swept over me.

CHAPTER 7
CAUGHT BETWEEN WORLDS

The men of Ulster returned to Emain victorious, but my father returned with barely a thread of breath connecting him to his life.

Have you ever been in a crowd cheering home an army? I stood pressed against my mother, submerged in the high voices of the women, and I heard like a bad string in a sweet harp the edge of anxiety shrilling through them all. We cheered for victory, but there was not one among us whose eyes did not search for a husband, a son, a father, a lover, even when all we could yet see were the bright banners above a dark moving mass of faceless men.

The king, riding at the head of his proud host, had hardly come into clear view when my mother gave a great cry. I peered up at her, smelling the wave of sour sweat that came on the heels of her fear, but I saw only her back. She was leaving me, thrusting her way through the noisy crowd back toward the gates. I called out to her, tried to push past the thronged bodies to follow and ran finally into the dimpled arms of Miach, Sencha's wife. Her gray braids hung like old ropes in front of my face as she bent to hold me.

"Stay here, little one. Your ma will be riding out to meet the army, and you cannot follow."

"Why is she going?" I demanded, and Miach's kind blue eyes slid away from my own.

"Cuchulainn is the champion of Ulster," she said. "He should have been riding by the king's side."

Ξ

The poets say now that my father had "not the place the point of a needle but had some hurt on it," and that is near to the truth. I thought he was dead when they carried him into Emain Macha, for how could a man survive such butchery? The sight of his mangled body froze my limbs with fear, so that they all—the men carrying him and my mother hurrying at their side—swept past me while I stood rooted to the ground. But Miach saw me and brought me to my father's side, explaining that he still lived.

It was Laeg told us how it had been, while my father lay silent and suffering with his wounds. Cuchulainn had not wasted his few men in head-on battle, but had harried the edges of Maeve's army day and night.

"He has such an arm on him, that throws farther than any other man and never misses, that with only his sling he caused such destruction that every man on the outer fringe feared constantly for his life," said Laeg. He gave that grin, the wolf grin, which had frightened me back in Muirthemne. "And then," he said, "betimes we would hitch up the chariot and cut through them in a great swathe, leaving the dead thick on the ground behind us, and none had speed to follow us."

At night Cuchulainn's hero-cry tore through the darkness, and by the light of morning so many lay dead on the ground that Maeve's army seemed to be melting away.

Day by day, Maeve's men became more nervous and demoralized, and soon she was ready to make terms. My father offered to fight a one-on-one combat each day. While they fought, her army could advance. But if Cuchulainn defeated Maeve's champion, they would have to make camp until the following day, and he would leave them in peace.

"At first Cuchulainn won his combats in minutes, so that Maeve's army crawled forward at an ant's pace," said Laeg. "But still no reinforcements came, and between combat and night patrols there was little rest to be had. Then Maeve began to cheat. She sent assassins into our camp by night and made a mockery of the rules of single combat.

"She sent twelve against him," Laeg told us, the anger hard in his eyes, "and claimed that since they were all of one family it would count as but one man. And still Cuchulainn prevailed, but it was long and weary work, and meantime the army advanced. And we learned afterward that while they were far ahead of us and Cuchulainn hard pressed, Maeve sent part of her army in a loop toward Cooley, and that is the arm that the young lads from Emain encountered. And the vengeance Cuchulainn took, when word came to us of their slaughter, is beyond anything I can describe. The wrath of the Morrigu herself would not have been more deadly."

Still my father suffered little hurt until he faced his final challenger.

"It was Ferdia who came at last," Laeg told my mother, the words so bitter in his mouth you would think it was poison he tasted. "Ferdia, his own sworn arms-brother, his fellow in training with Scathach. And I swear," he said, "it was not Ferdia's strength and skill in arms but his betrayal that cut the Hound to the quick. Nothing would have turned him against Ferdia—not the riches Maeve offered, nor the promise of her daughter, nor the taunts and threats of her satirists either."

They fought for three days, and each morning my father tried to turn Ferdia from the deadly path he had chosen, but it could not be done. And Ferdia, who had learned so many of the same feats and tricks as my father, was a fierce opponent. "Never have I seen men so wounded and fighting still," said Laeg. "From dawn till dark they hacked at each other, until their bodies ran red with blood and the ground beneath them was slick with it. At times I had to goad and mock Cuchulainn, to stir up his strength and anger, yet it was weeping with pity I was, for all the hurts that were upon him."

When they fought in the River Dee, at the ford they now call Ath Ferdia, it was clear that both men were near to death. Only in the last extremity did my father call for the Gae Bolga, his deadliest spear. And when my father finally killed Ferdia, launching the Gae Bolga from under the water with his foot and ramming it up under Ferdia's iron apron, it is then he fell down weeping for the death of his friend and began to sink into a stupor from his wounds and sorrow and exhaustion.

Laeg managed to rouse him and drag him away from the open riverbank to safety, and there my father lay, unable to bear even the weight of a cloth upon his wounds, until the sounds of battle roused him. The men of Ulster had come at last, and when Cuchulainn heard the cry of the Ochain, Conchobor's magic shield, his anger came upon him and he rose up despite his injuries, and fought alongside his people until Maeve's army was utterly smashed.

He had not so much as lifted his head since.

᚛

The long months that my father lay in the Speckled House—for he had roused only long enough to insist he be taken to sleep there among the weapons and shields of the Red Branch—were the strangest I had yet known. To be sure, there was grieving for the dead and doctoring for the living, but life soon returned to its normal bustle for everyone, it seemed, except me. My mother spent her days at my father's side, trying to coax him out of the uncanny sleep that held him suspended between the world of the living and that of the dead. And just as my father neither died nor woke, so his wounds did not fester, but neither did they heal.

And I—I hung suspended also. I had no nurse, no chores, no lessons. For the first time I missed old Tullia, for all her fussy protectiveness. She would have scolded my idleness and found some task to keep me occupied. As it was, I had Fintan for company. Of course there were other children there, and I did sometimes join in their games, but I believe there was something—perhaps awe of my father's state, or the druid's raven on my shoulder—that made them wary of me, for I made no true friends.

We had lit the Beltane fires a couple of weeks before the army's return. It hadn't been much of a Beltane, not with so many of the men gone and more than a few women too, but we had put a brave show on it and honored the sun's return as best we could.

By high summer my father was no better, and for once at Lughnasadh the games and contests were all won by other men. My mother left the Speckled House for the whole day to take me there, and she tried her best to hide her worries for my sake. "It is Lugh of the Long Hand your father loves above all gods," she said. "It would not do for you to come all the way to Emain and miss his great festival. I promise you, you will never see the like in Muirthemne."

We passed the day in a glorious confusion of color, noise and smell. The sun shone hot in a clear sky and lit up the bright clothing we all wore to celebrate first harvest. Even the farmers and craftsmen sported ribbons and sashes to add color to their plain tunics, while their women wove flowers into their hair and wrapped swatches of dyed cloth around their waists. We had to yell to hear each other, for all around us people called to their friends, onlookers cheered the games, bards told their tales in voices that carried halfway across a field, traders haggled over their wares, musicians piped and drummed. People danced and laughed and fought and drank and ate a seemingly endless supply of food. The wafted smells of roasting meat, fresh-baked bread and barley beer mingled with the sharper odors of sweat and manure until I was light-headed with breathing them.

I was in a silly mood, jigging and gamboling about my mother like a pup on its first hunt. She only laughed at me, though, and even caught my hands and swung me into the air. I suppose we both exaggerated our high spirits that day. It had been too long since there was anything to laugh about.

But when I whirled about to see Cathbad's feathered cloak in front of me, I was embarrassed at my foolishness. I felt my cheeks grow hot as his eyes rested on me. He exchanged greetings with my mother, and then he studied me again.

"How old are you, Luaine?"

A spring baby, I added to my count of years each Beltane. "This is my eighth summer," I confessed. Too old for such nonsense, I imagined his voice saying.

Of course he said no such thing. All around me, grown men and women were acting just as giddy. In the right place, laughter honors the gods as well as solemnity. Cathbad turned to my mother.

"A child that age should be starting her education and training, Emer, surely."

My mother looked startled, then flustered. "Yes, Cathbad, of course. At home she has begun her training already."

It was quite true. I may have been raised in the quiet countryside of Muirthemne, but my mother, the druid's daughter, saw to it that my education was not neglected.

Of women's arts, I had already started to learn the needlework: spinning and weaving, sewing and embroidery. These my mother taught me herself, for her own needle was renowned. I never grew to love the work as she did—though I did enjoy the embroidery, the colors taking shape and meaning under my fingers—but thanks to her efforts, I eventually became a fast and precise seamstress. I had also begun learning household management. Though we had servants, I would still have to learn what each task was, how to do it properly and when it should occur, so that I would be able to oversee my own household one day. So far my training had consisted mostly of being sent to help with various chores, but in the years to come I would spend many weeks with our cook, learning how the foods were stored, how to take inventory and calculate how long supplies would last, how to tell what was fresh and succulent, how to prepare dishes, how to plan menus for a feast or great gathering. I would pass as many days following the housekeeper, learning everything from how to bank the peat fire to hold heat through the night, to how to keep moths from the blanket chests and bugs from our mattresses.

The household tasks I endured and learned, but with little enthusiasm. Riding and horse husbandry I loved better, and better still the lessons I had started in singing and poetry. Like most of the great families, we had our own poet. It is Lasair, in fact, who is responsible for some of the more outrageous verses about my father. He must have been delighted to have such a man for a patron, for he was never lacking for material or stuck with the task of singing undeserved praises. When he wasn't traveling after Cuchulainn, he was my teacher, setting me to learn by heart the long histories of Ireland, the stories of our gods and goddesses and kings and champions. He taught me the proper forms of poetry as well as the art of riddles, rhetoric and repartee.

But a season and more had passed since we had left Dun Dealgan, and I heard Cathbad say to Emer, "It is not good for her to spend so much time alone. And who can say when your life at home will resume? There are many noble families who would gladly foster her."

It was common for girls to be fostered at my age, though it was most often boys who were sent to be instructed by uncles or allies. But my mother shook her head, and I knew by the stubborn lift of her chin that not even the chief druid would prevail over her in this matter.

"No, I'll not send my only living child away. Not now. We need each other now."

The rush of love and pride I felt was ferocious, almost painful. I had felt myself a burden and thought she must begrudge the childish needs that took her from my father's side. But she would not have it so. I pressed as close beside her as I could and still stand straight, as straight as Emer herself.

The old druid's eyes crinkled in unexpected amusement. "I didn't really suppose you would. Come and speak to me after the festival, and we'll see what can be done here in Emain." And he strode off in a swirl of colors.

That evening, for the first time, I saw the serious side of Lughnasadh. I should have realized Cathbad would not don his robe of office to oversee a noisy party. We gathered on the shores of the little lake I had glimpsed from the embankments of Emain, and I watched as Cathbad and two other druids stood in the golden slanting light and chanted a long hypnotic prayer. A young bull was led to the altar, and the sacrificer slipped the knife in so expertly that the calf barely seemed to know he had been hurt, but stood quietly, his blood rushing into the great basin, until his knees folded under him and he sank slowly to the ground. Acrid smoke billowed up from the fire as his blood was sprinkled on the flames: blood carried up to the heavens, blood seeping down to the depths of the earth. Life shared with those who live above, below and beyond our own world. And then, at a word from Cathbad, those with special prayers or messages for the god stepped forward to the very edge of the water.

My mother went then, with the others. I could not hear what she whispered to the god, but I knew what she asked. And as the last rays of the sun lit up the bronze water, she removed the wide golden band that wrapped her bare arm and cast it far out over the still surface of the lake.

Of the finest metalwork, my mother's favorite, that armband was. The great god Lugh was a patron of all skills and craftsmanship. He would appreciate its worth.

Ξ

Of course the chief druid was not about to concern himself with cookery lessons. It was a wonder to me that he concerned himself with my welfare at all. But he did allow me to come to the lessons held every morning for the sons of the noble families in Emain. Girls could be taught too, if their parents wished it, but we were generally given private lessons within the family grouping. Boys in their first stirrings of manhood are considered difficult enough to teach, I suppose, without the distraction of young females at their side!

In any case, I was too young to excite any attention at all from the bigger boys, and there was certainly room for me. Each class was a painful reminder of the death of the boy troop, for although Follaman, Conchobor's son who led the boys, had made the youngest ones stay back, there were none past the age of thirteen left to teach. We made a small group, rarely more than ten.

I went every morning. I believe I was the only one who did, for these were warriors' sons, destined for the sword and the spear, and most would take any excuse to miss their lessons. But I sat on the fringes of the restless, often reluctant, boys and listened as I never had before. The vastness of all there was to know was overwhelming: not only our histories, but calculation, star reading, navigation, herb lore and healing, natural and human law. Cathbad's druids shared teaching duties, and as one or another would take the class, I came to see that each had his own deep pool of knowledge. It's little enough I understood of what they said, but I ate up their words like a greedy nestling.

CHAPTER 8
THE WOMAN OF THE SIDHE

My father lay in the Speckled House, and the seasons turned. When the golden leaves of the orchards began to drift down, and the first night frost left the grass stiff and white at dawn, harvest took on an urgency that made the autumn air hum with purpose. Apples, grain, turnips—anything that would keep was gathered and stored, and anything that wouldn't was eaten. The peat cutters stacked their dried bricks into huge mounds, and when the herdsmen began bringing the cattle and sheep in from summer pasture and the air grew sharp with the tang of slaughter and smoke, I realized with a start that Samhain was only days away.

I was frightened of Samhain. I expect all children are, at that moment when every fire and lamp is put out, and we stand so alone in the dark, so close to the Otherworld we feel its very breath on our necks. When the druids finally finished their chants and prayers and offerings and lit the Winter Fire, it was not only children who felt a surge of relief.

Samhain in Emain Macha was a huge event. Besides the rush to have all in readiness for the dark season, besides the ceremony itself, there was a great gathering of all the chieftains and lesser kings of Ulster. It was the greatest feast of the year, when Conchobor exchanged pledges with his sworn men and rewarded his champions. And then, in the days that followed, the Wise Ones would sit in judgment, to hear peoples' claims and disputes.

But I saw neither feast nor fire, for my mother would not leave the Speckled House from the moment the sun began its long afternoon descent down the slope of the sky. Samhain would not begin until sundown, but Emer was taking no chances. With the veil between worlds becoming so thin, she said, the spirits of the dead and people of the Sidhe could intermingle freely with ourselves, and she feared my father's spirit might forsake us and slip away.

"He is not altogether in this world as it is, Luaine," she explained. "Even Cathbad cannot say what holds him to life. But if he were to leave us this night, and I not there to plead and fight for him to stay, the blame and grief would be with me to the end of my days."

I remembered what she had said—how we needed each other— and resolved to sit vigil too. It was, in any case, better than wandering alone among the crowds of people filling the settlement.

It was an eerie sight, my father laid out on a pallet amidst the bristling paraphernalia of war. The walls were hung with shields of bronze, leather and wood, each painted or embossed with its owner's device. Spears and swords thrust out from barrels. Certain weapons were given pride of place, carefully displayed: I recognized Conchobor's famous shield, and my father's massive barbed spear, the Gae Bolga. Those lethal barbs, hidden within the shaft, had killed Ferdia, and as I looked upon it I imagined for the first time, not my father's prowess to wield such a thing, but the ruin it must make of a man's body. The house was utterly silent—yet it seemed the air rang with the clash and riot of fighting. And there was Cuchulainn, his face so pale but for the livid wounds, the rents in his body hidden by the rich coverlet tented over him.

Servants felt it too, that eeriness. At dinnertime they brought our food in silence, eyes averted, and all but bolted for the door.

It was a raw windy day, the gusts stripping leaves off the trees and bringing sudden spatters of rain that blew over as quickly as they began. There would be neither star nor moonlight this Samhain. As darkness fell and people made their way to the hillside fire, the busy noise of Emain Macha was silenced. Now we could hear the soughing voice of the air and feel its chill as it whistled through the cracks in the heavy door and seeped in between wall and thatch. My mother lit candles and set them at my father's head, and our shadows jumped and shrank in their wavering light.

My father's lips moved, and he muttered in his sleep. My mother bent patiently to hear, as she had done so many times before, but there was no message for her in his restless whispers. She slipped her hand under the coverlet and wrapped her fingers around his shield-hand—the one place that had been protected from all injury.

What would she do when the time came to kill the summer light, I wondered. She would not want to leave my father to the dark—but how could we relight our lamps, sitting here alone? The ritual was both a promise to the people and a reminder to the spirit of the sun, that the dark season would not last forever but turn again to light and warmth. It was an act of faith, and I could not guess what might happen if we refused it.

"Cathbad will send an apprentice with a torch from the sacred fire," my mother remarked, as if I had spoken aloud. Her voice was calm, her face peaceful as she turned to me. "You needn't fear the dark time, dove. Cathbad has woven spells of protection about this house, and we are strong and full of life. The spirits cannot harm us. My fear is only for Cuchulainn. Many strong warriors are dead on his account. He killed in honor, but there may yet be some restless dead who hunger for revenge."

A gruesome picture came to my mind: the shriveled trophy heads that hung in the House of the Red Branch coming to life, calling my father's name.

The night wore on, and my mother sat now with a blanket drawn about her against the cold, and I snuggled into the little bed that had been made for me, though I was determined not to sleep. At last the gong rang out, signaling the End of the Light, and my mother blew out the candles, the faint light fading to thickest black as one by one they died.

Eyes open, eyes shut; it made no difference. The dark was a dense shroud that seemed to muffle sound as well as sight. But as time passed, and no disembodied heads appeared, the tension strung through my body gradually gave way to fatigue. My eyes closed, and I drifted.

The oak door banged open with a force that thudded through the entire structure and rattled the shields. I jolted upright, crying aloud, and heard my mother's voice ringing out with mine. Hearts thudding, we strained our eyes into the black as a cold wind swirled around us.

"It's only the wind," my mother assured me. Her voice was firm and confident, and I heard her grope her way carefully to the door and force it closed. "Go back to sleep, Luaine. It's nothing, just the wind, and the light will come soon."

It was the first time I had known my mother's words to be false. Not that she lied, not deliberately. But she was wrong. It wasn't the wind. Something had entered the Speckled House. It sat with us now in the dark.

Ξ

I cannot say now, looking back to the child I was, if it was awe or a reluctance to alarm my mother that stilled my tongue. But I said nothing and waited in silence, for I knew it was no gory head that had floated in on the wind. The presence in the room was foreign, but it was not evil.

I did not know I could sense such things until that moment. And when Cathbad's young man finally pushed open the door and the blaze of his torch thrust into the corners of the room, I knew—as did he with his druid's eyes—that it was no human woman sitting there so quietly at my father's other side. She was one of the Tuatha Da Danaan—a woman of the Sidhe. I stared in wonder, and she smiled at me, acknowledging my recognition. It was as the poets said: She had the appearance of an earthly woman. Yet there was no mistaking what she was.

At least not for me. As the apprentice touched his forehead in respectful greeting, my mother spoke up sharply.

"And who are you at all? Why do you come sneaking by night to my husband's sickbed?"

I wondered at her tone. She was badly frightened, covering it with bluster.

The woman was Liban, and she brought the strangest message.

"It is for my sister, Fand, I have come to this man. For Manannan, Son of the Sea, is no longer her husband, and her love has fallen on Cuchulainn. And the coming of Cuchulainn would bring great joy to her heart."

The anger in my mother was a bristling heat in the room. I thought she might attack the woman with her bare hands, until Liban's next words caught her startled attention.

"It is not long his sickness would be, if Cuchulainn would come to the Happy Plain. He will be healed, and what is lost of his strength will be given back to him again. It is Fand and myself will cure his sickness and wake him from his long sleep."

The silence stretched on, and still my mother did not speak. She didn't seem to know where to look, or what to do with herself. I was too young to understand the turmoil of emotions warring within her, but I could see how she struggled to keep her composure.

She turned to Cathbad's apprentice and told him to take me to the Royal House.

"You go to bed now, Luaine. I must speak with Liban."

It was a voice that brooked no argument. I pulled my cloak tight about my shoulders and followed the young man out the door.

☰

We left Emain Macha the next day, after another hurried preparation. I don't suppose my mother was anxious to endure everyone's curious eyes and prying questions. I can only imagine what it cost her to swallow her pride and jealousy and give my father to another woman, not knowing if he would ever return. She was distant that morning, her face set in a mask, her eyes hiding something close to grief.

Doubtless there had been other women before Fand. If you believe the bards, Cuchulainn lay with half the women of Ireland. But if he did, it was far from home, and always he gave Emer pride of place. There had never been any question of losing him.

So it was a bleak setting off we had, on a dark and drizzly day. I remember wondering how Liban had transported my father back to her Otherworld home. Had she carried him in her arms? Turned him to vapor and vanished down one of the deep rock clefts that lead to the land of the Sidhe?

The wind was cold, and I was glad when we entered the humpy wooded hills that fan west from the Cooley Mountains. The broad track from Emain Macha narrowed to thread its way through oak and hawthorn trees, and I remember the clatter of the chariot seemed so loud in that shadowy world. But then we emerged onto a long bare slope with a little rushing creek at its feet—and there, where the track turned aside to avoid the water, stood the king's chariot. My mother and Berach kicked their horses forward, no doubt expecting nothing but a broken wheel or similar trouble, and without thinking, my driver followed.

And there was Deirdriu. She lay sprawled at the foot of a great standing stone, her skull smashed, her silken hair clotted with blood and brains. Her lovely face gone. Conchobor and Eoghan were there. I heard their voices, angry and confused, but I never gave them a glance. My eyes were trapped, stuck like a fly in pine resin, on the terrible sight.

Conchobor had been taking her to Eoghan's dun, but Deirdriu had held to her vow. She killed herself, driving her head against the Old Ones' stone as the chariot flew by.

I had been chilled already, the wind nipping my fingers and nose as we traveled, but now I shivered and could not stop. But my mother came back to herself then, and back to me. She laid her hand over my eyes and drew me away, against her own chest. She wrapped her arms around me and chafed my hands, and then she pulled me onto her own red mare.

"Come now, dove. We'll go home," she said, and the word sounded so sweet it filled me with longing.

I will never forget how it looked when we finally emerged from the hummocky north country and looked down on the long slope of the Muirthemne plain. The autumn sun suddenly sailed free of the clouds to light up the patchwork fields, as if the earth were giving up a harvest of jewels. The wind carried just a hint of the sea—the smell of home—and it seemed all the troubles and horror and fear we had had were eased, and I could be a little girl again.

Chapter 9
Dun Dealgan

My father spent one month in the land of the Sidhe, and then one day he walked in our door as strong and full of life as ever before.

Emer and I flung ourselves at him, and he laughed and held his arms wide so he could hold us both at once. All that day my mother could not stop looking at him, her eyes shining with the wonder of it. "Not even a scar," she marveled, stroking her hand along his arm. "Not the tiniest mark."

At first it seemed like everything was back to normal. Only slowly did I notice the tension in the silences, the forced quality of the talk, the way my father would seek out solitude and my mother's unhappiness when he did so.

Then came a morning when my mother blazed around the house in a white fury, gathering her women all about her and arming each with a knife sharpened to a murderous edge. I could get no hint of what drove her—she snapped at Tullia to keep me at home and they all swept off toward the strand.

I did think of defying Tullia—she was old, and at eight I could already outrun her—but my mother's dark rage would not have brooked it. So I waited, in an agony of confusion and anxiety, and when at last I saw my parents making their way home together, and neither one visibly bloody, I hoped that our happiness at Dun Dealgan would finally be restored.

But it was not. It was only some weeks later, after a visit from Cathbad, that the strange uneasiness in our family melted away.

I did not understand what had actually happened until long after, when I pried the story from one of my mother's women. My father had come home, but he could not forget the woman of the Sidhe who had healed him. And Fand loved him still as well. So they arranged to meet on Baile's Strand, but my mother discovered their rendezvous and was overcome with jealousy.

Yet when she arrived there and looked on Fand, her heart changed. She saw that Fand's yearning for my father was as strong as her own, and the rage melted away into sorrow.

She put down her bright knives, stood before the woman who loved her husband, and she said, "I will give him up to you."

But it was Fand who released her claim to Cuchulainn and returned to her husband Manannan, and to her own shining country. For, as she said to Emer, "The man is yours, and you are worthy." And Cathbad, in his turn, mixed for my parents a draught of forgetfulness, the way my father would forget his longing for Fand, and my mother forget her jealousy.

≡

When Cathbad came to Dun Dealgan with the draught for my parents, he brought something for me as well: he brought Fintan. I count it the most valuable gift I have ever received, or am ever likely to.

"He has been restless since you left, Luaine," he said, hoisting down the wicker travel cage from a cart with slow care. "I believe he is meant to stay with you." And indeed, when Cathbad opened the cage door and Fintan waddled through, he did not hesitate but launched himself straight toward my shoulder. I braced myself against his ungainly landing and laughed as he set straight to nibbling at my ear.

Tullia's call interrupted our reunion.

"It seems you are wanted," said Cathbad gravely.

I sighed. "I am to help with the grinding." Grinding grain is a laborious business, and the person who spends an afternoon cranking the heavy millstones wakes up with an ache across her shoulders to prove it. I was not big enough to take my turn at grinding, but was put to work scooping the dusty meal into sacks nearly as big as myself. It was not my favorite job.

"I am glad to see you working alongside your people," Cathbad remarked. "One should never be too proud to work."

I colored, for in truth it rankled me to be set to menial tasks in the kitchen, and I a chieftain's daughter.

"Sir," I ventured. I wasn't sure if I was allowed to question the teaching of the chief druid, but I did it anyway. He cocked an eyebrow at me. "I don't understand. How is it wrong, to be proud?" Pride was the life-blood of our warriors and noble women—their spur to great accomplishments, the wellspring of their courage. I had not thought there could be any such thing as "too proud."

Now both eyebrows raised, and I braced myself for the clout on the head my impudence might have earned. Instead I got one of his slow nods.

"Look to your mother," he said. "She is as proud a woman as walks Ireland. Yet she did not hesitate in Celthair's dun to set her hands to work the servants quailed from. Am I not correct?"

I nodded, trying to grasp his lesson.

"When laziness, or weakness, or meanness hides behind pride, it is like a rich cloak used to cover filthy rags. True pride reflects true worth. Your mother knows the difference."

Tullia's voice came again.

"Go now, to your grinding," said Cathbad. "Tell them the chief druid said Fintan is to keep you company."

I turned to go, then spun back one last time. Fintan squawked irritably as he overbalanced first one way, then the other, and the clenching grip of his talons made me feel his annoyance right through my heavy winter tunic. But my time in Emain Macha had changed me. I was no longer such a little girl that I did not know how to receive a gift.

"I thank you, Cathbad, for bringing Fintan to me," I said. "I promise I will care for him well."

I worked harder that day and complained less. I took pride in my work.

Ξ

That winter my training began in earnest. I was no longer playing at sewing or getting underfoot in the scullery; I was expected to work carefully and with some skill. Some days I was kept so busy I was grateful to have Fin as my excuse for some free time. Even after I had stopped shutting him inside except at night, I insisted that Cathbad expected me to spend time with Fintan every day. Fin expected it, in any case. He was always waiting for me when I came, and I can chart my growing into womanhood by the way I looked forward to my rambles with Fin. At first they brought me a chance to return to the childish freedom I had known; later it was the privacy and solitude I was grateful for.

And then there was Eirnin. My mother must have taken Cathbad's words about my education seriously, for she went herself to speak with the druid, traveling in wintertime across the plain of Bregia to her childhood home. He had been her own tutor, back when he was merely old rather than ancient. She had long labor to persuade him to come to us at Muirthemne, but early that spring he appeared at our gates with an ox-pulled wagon piled high with his possessions, and he stayed at Dun Dealgan until his death.

He was the oldest man I had ever seen—and the grouchiest. At first I could see nothing but that: he was all gray beard and stringy hands and sunken eyes and glaring impatience. Unlike the servants and my other teachers, he did not smile and praise me when my answer was right; he only set me harder questions and waited malevolently to pounce on my least mistake. He made my stomach twist into knots, with his glittery eye and harsh words.

I hated him. But as I began to see the worlds Eirnin could unlock for me, my feelings changed.

The turning point was the Ogham. I was waiting for Eirnin in the stuffy back room that served as a classroom, feeling my stomach jump and complain, wishing I could be anywhere else. The minutes stretched on, until it was I who was impatient, and I began to wonder what puzzles he would set me that day. Like my mother, I have a competitive mind. I did not—and do not to this day—like even a druid to get the better of me.

Eirnin shuffled into the room at last, clattering with every step. His arms were filled with a bundle of pale sticks, each as big around as my wrist and over half my height. He dumped them onto the table, selected one and laid it before me.

"Do you know what this is?" His pale eyes glowered at me under great sprouting eyebrows.

I looked at the stick in front of me. It was peeled and polished smooth, so that the rounded back felt almost silky in my hands. The front was carved to have two flat sides that met at a square angle. This long square edge was marked with clusters of notches: little brown lines tilted this way and that, marching up the wood. They formed no picture, and if they were decorative it was a poor attempt, for they had no flow or grace of composition.

I shook my head, so intrigued I forgot to be nervous. "No, sir. What are the marks for?"

Perhaps he saw, when I looked up at him, that he had ignited something, for he grinned at me, showing long yellow teeth. "They make a message. Each mark has its own pattern, its own meaning. Learn the marks, and you will know the message."

I ran my hand over the row wonderingly. Like little people calling to me, I thought, only their voices are silent.

It was hard to take my eyes away, to look back at Eirnin. He too was silent, waiting.

"Teach me," I said. I had never wanted anything so badly.

☰

Two weeks later, I wanted to take those sticks and hurl them into a fire.

It was impossibly complicated. There were twenty different patterns of notches, making twenty different symbols. A single symbol was distinguished not only by the number of notches (one to five) but by their angle and by whether they crossed or stayed to one side of the midline. And each symbol represented a tree: birch, rowan, alder and so on. This much I managed to grasp, learning a few more symbols each day until I could "read" them from the bottom to the top of each of Eirnin's sticks.

"But, sir," I finally asked, having completed this task, "how can a list of trees be a message?"

"Ah. The trees are just their names. Each symbol also makes a sound, and the sounds together make the message."

"The trees are just their names?" Surely I had misunderstood.

"Eight of the trees, to be precise, give their names directly to the symbols. The other symbols have names which are associated with the trees."

My mind balked, and I shouted in my frustration. "Where is the use in that?" All I could think was how hard I had worked to memorize those hateful trees, apparently for nothing.

Eirnin pressed his lips into a tight line. He gathered up his Ogham sticks and stalked out of the room, leaving me to war within myself between indignation and my own desire to learn.

The next day I apologized. Eirnin made me wait one more day, and then we began on the sounds that went with each symbol.

Years later I learned that the tree names do have a purpose of their own. The druids will teach the Ogham to any likely student, but the sacred symbology of the trees is for their initiates only. So the system is not so pointless as it once seemed to an impatient girl.

☰

I had no brothers or sisters. Just before Maeve's invasion, my mother had lost another baby boy: Born before the swell of her belly could be seen under her skirts, he was far too tiny to live. Her first boy, born when I was barely old enough to remember, had been healthy and strong. He had just started to smile, beaming and dimpling at anything that caught his eye, when he died in his sleep one afternoon for no reason at all. I'm told the nurse who found him cold and lifeless left Dun Dealgan with only the clothes on her back rather than face Cuchulainn after such news. I was old enough now to realize that my father longed for a son. He had a great gift, and he looked to pass it on.

So when he announced, early in my tenth year, that my training should include the arts of war, I confess I had a sudden vision of myself fighting at my father's side, the two of us shining with glory. There are women warriors among our people who are counted among the great: Scathach, mighty in skill and magic, who trained my father; and her rival Aoife, the great warrior queen. Queen Maeve herself rode into battle with her troops and was a mighty figure among them. I saw myself in a chariot bristling with weapons, thundering across a plain, the hero light about me…

My mother shot Cuchulainn a look from under her eyebrows. "What is this, then, Cuchulainn?" Doubtless she had glimpsed the same vision and had a rather different reaction.

But he said only, "It is well for a woman to know the sword as well as the needle. The time may arise when she has need to defend herself or her children." Emer could not argue against the reason of his words. Indeed, she herself, like most noble women, had some training with the sword.

For myself, I was eager to start. How not? I was Cuchulainn's daughter.

≡

If many girls have some arms training, few receive it from the likes of Berach. My father's arms master had trained a good number of the men in my father's troops, and proven himself in many a battle too.

This my father told me as he led me to the training ground that had been set up behind the house. "And while you are under his tutelage," he reminded me, "you will call him Master."

Berach was a formidable man, especially from the vantage point of a child. The first thing I encountered was a pair of massive red hands, big-knuckled, resting one atop the other on the pommel of the long sword that thrust down into the earth. My eyes traveled up along the ropy scarred arms, heavily furred with copper hair. When they reached his face—a face like an ax-head it was, broad and weathered with a thick neck and jaw, pale cold eyes and a bristling mustache to match the flaming orange of his hair—he smiled and bowed.

"Mistress Luaine." Oddly, the smile changed his looks a great deal, adding warmth and good humor to the stony features. I understood why my father had chosen this man. He was hard as iron, but I trusted him right away.

We got on well, Berach and I, and I think he was pleased at my progress. Strong and well-coordinated for my age, nimble on my feet, I did not fear the sting of the flat side of his blade or to lose my wind in a fall. I did not want him to think he need baby me for being a girl, so even when the hurt made me howl and cry, I would make myself get up and wipe the snot from my face and try again.

For about a year I used a wooden practice sword and shield. Then I graduated to a plain iron blade, its edge blunted for practice, and a shield bossed in bronze. Iron was much heavier than wood, I discovered, and by the end of our first session my arms burned and trembled with exertion. My mother came to watch me that day. She shook her head at the sight of me as I trudged off the field, streaked all over with sweat and mud. I wondered at first was she displeased, but then she laughed and put her arm around my shoulders. "You are a tough little nut," she said, and I took it as high praise.

Ξ

My father did not come to the training ground until the spring of my twelfth birthday, and when he did it was not to watch me train but to enter the ring with me. He took a wooden sword from the barrel that held our training arms and said mildly, "Well then, Luaine, come and show me how you are getting on." Nothing more—yet I knew, deep in my bones, that this was a test. He made me show him the strokes I had learned as well as the defenses and the positions of the shield; I recited for him how each would be used, and I could tell Berach was pleased with me. And then my father set me to spar. He was careful, not pressing me past my abilities but making me work my very hardest, so that by the time we were done I could scarce draw air into my lungs.

I stood there, gasping for breath, wiping the sweat off my forehead, and I saw in his eyes that my best had not been enough. My father had been only seven when he bested all the boys in the Emain Macha playing field. I would not be following in his footsteps.

Then he smiled at me, and his face showed only pleasure. "You have earned your sword, Luaine. It's proud I am of you this day." And he went to a bundle he had left lying by the wattle fence, and drew out the beautiful tooled scabbard I had worn as a little girl careening off to Emain Macha in a chariot. Berach had stored it away on our safe return, but now, once again, my father buckled it around me. This time it hung at my side as if it belonged there. It's strange, but I knew that he spoke truth. I had done well, and he *was* proud of me. Only he was sad to have no heir to his brilliance.

Cuchulainn turned from me then and threw his arm around Berach; the two ambled off deep in talk. I watched them walk together for a bit, then I limped over to the barrel and tossed in my training sword. I ladled out water from the trough and poured it over my head.

"That's good, little chick."

The voice was insolent, even hostile. I glanced around quickly and saw it belonged to the man who came after our sessions to gather up the weapons and store them away. He looked at me with a sneer that made my cheeks burn hot.

"Your mighty da give you a little gift, did he? And a fine prize for a young chick, it is too. Something wasted on a bit of a girl like you, though." He chewed at his mustache, considering me, and then suddenly he was up close against me, the odor of ale and sweat rank in my face.

"But that's all right, isn't it?" he breathed. "You won't be a girl much longer, and soon enough your prize will go to a man who knows what to do with it." His face twisted into a gap-toothed leer, and his hand grabbed the slim curve of my behind and pulled me against him.

I was speechless with the shock of it. But the heat that roared into life within me was immediate and searing. Flames licked at the inside of my skull, and the world around me darkened and receded. All I could see was the shining point of my blade where it pressed against his neck. I had no memory of grasping for it. The rage throbbed through me, and with it the desire to push the silvery weapon through his white flesh and release his blood. I was only vaguely aware that his hand had dropped away from my body and that he stood stock-still against the fence.

I forced my eyes upward, to his face, pasty now with fear.

"You had best not have the bad judgment to touch me or even speak to me again." The words were spoken from my lips, but they seemed to come from someone else—someone older. Someone with power. "For as you see, young as I am I do not wear this sword as an ornament. But if you bother me in the least way again, it's the Hound himself will be baying after you, and I promise you will not live to bother me one more time."

He swallowed, and I let the point of the sword ride up and down with the knob of his throat.

"Get out of here," I said, and he gathered up his legs and ran.

I was left weak and shaky, as though I had been ill. And I was desperate to be alone, for I was confused—both shamed and elated by what had happened. Ignoring my dirty clothes and the rest of the day's lessons, I hurried to the stables and helped myself to the lazy old horse I had learned to ride on. It was a long walk to the bay where the River Nith empties into the sea, but there is nothing like the steady rhythmic rush of the ocean for thinking.

I had made a full-grown man afraid of me. And though there was nothing so remarkable about what I had done—I had used my sword as I had been taught and threatened him with my father's retribution, the way any child might—I could not shake the feeling that it had not really been me who had done these things. I could not remember *intending* to act or speak, but I had done so all the same, with an assurance I had never known. Was it perhaps my own version of the warrior's frenzy that made me act so? I remembered again the rush of heat to my head, enough, it seemed, to make the roots of my hair catch fire. Did my father feel that too, and when the heat ebbed away did it leave him feeling so empty?

That day I felt the first stirrings of my own power and began the journey away from childhood.

CHAPTER 10
THE MAKING OF A MAIDEN

Shall I tell you more about Fintan? Perhaps you have wondered why I set such store by a mere animal.

It is only slowly I discovered what Fintan—or rather Fintan and I together—could do, and I think now that Cathbad was wise to let us develop our abilities naturally rather than trying to teach me. I knew, of course, that the druids find auguries and omens in the calls and flights of birds. I thought that was what Cathbad meant when he said that Fin was not "ordinary." But any bird will do for that sort of crude soothsaying.

I had always talked to Fin. I was a lonely, worried little girl when we met in Emain Macha, and I would have poured out my heart to a caterpillar. But after he had been with me in Dun Dealgan for some time, I began to see that he understood at least some of what I said and was able to respond in his own way. If I asked did he want to go down to the strand, he would fly off in that direction and wait for me at the head of the path where it started its steep descent. Or if he was not inclined to agree, he might waddle about on his perch to set his back against me, or fly in another direction and call as if to say, "No! Let's head over to the horse pasture so I can hunt for dung beetles." He responded to my moods too, and when I was upset would rattle softly in his throat and press up against me.

We continued like that for a long time, and I not really noticing how the link between our minds grew steadily stronger, how

Fintan's understanding grew far beyond the few words a dog, say, may come to recognize. It unsettled Tullia, though. "You talk to that bird as if it were a person," she would say, her voice scolding. She thought it high time I gave up such childish fancies. But if she had known the truth of it, she would have held her tongue for fear of him.

The truth is, Fin is a Messenger. The day I discovered it was one of the rare times Fin was not waiting for me when I came for him. I remember feeling frightened when I didn't find him in any of his favorite places—not outside the kitchens, or in the rafters of the horse barn, or hunkered on the point of our roof like a brooding black sentinel. "He comes and goes as he pleases," Cathbad's voice reminded me, but oh—what if he had gone for good? I stood on the embankment facing north and whistled for him, wondering if he might have returned to Emain Macha, but then his raucous call turned me around to see him sailing in from the east, riding the sea breeze.

It was one of a string of fine late-summer afternoons, and after several days with no rain the plain was dry and springy under-foot. I was tired, body and mind, having been worked as hard by my tutors as by Berach. Lasair and Eirnin must have entered into a contest of their own, I thought, to see who could stuff the most knowledge into my head. It rang now with snatches of song and poetry, chanted histories and long recited lists, all scrambled together.

"We won't go far today, Fin." Dun Dealgan was built on a hill that gave views to the horizon in every direction, but I soon found a little hollow, free of gorse and thistle, that would keep me out of Tullia's sight. I threw myself down with my face tipped up to the sun, and Fin settled beside me. Closing my eyes, I looked up through red-lit eyelids, watching the little patterns and lights that played through my vision when I screwed up my eyes and then released them. The sweet grassy smell of the meadow rose around me. I flipped over on to my stomach, folded my arms under my head and let myself drowse.

The liquid call of a lark spiraled up into the air, too beautiful to ignore. I turned lazily to Fin. "No offense intended," I joked, "but your own voice is sadly lacking by comparison. Perhaps some tutoring for yourself…"

He was preening his feathers, paying me no mind at all. One great black wing was stretched out across my vision, as he craned his neck behind to reach the base of his tail. The white feather hung stark against the black, leaping into the foreground, making its backdrop recede and blur. I lay watching it, fascinated as before with the startling effect of the contrast. I began to see more than a simple white patch: the intricate interlocking pattern of the ribs, the graceful line of the quill, the downy fluff at the base. Fin flexed the wing, and the white feather was rippled by blue shadow, and then it glowed again in the sun. Ripples and gleams of sunlight…

The ripples spread out as far as I could see, blue topped with frothy white. I lay relaxed, dreamy, enjoying the breeze in my hair and the sparkling pattern before my eyes. I gave the sight no more thought than the lights I had made dance on my closed eyelids—until I saw the birds. Sea birds, wheeling and crying below me! Around me. Gulls and gannets and terns and below us all the blue ripples were ocean. When I raised my eyes I saw rims of land like two arms spread out to the sea, dark hills rising to my left, a flat green spit on the right, and I recognized our own bay.

There were ships—three ships—cresting the horizon. I had never seen one before, but even from this strange high perspective it was obvious what they were. Sailing ships, coming to our shore.

With a gasp, I tore my eyes away and sat up. The change of perspective made me dizzy, so much green, too close, too solid. A secret, Cathbad had called Fintan's white feather. Now I had glimpsed its full meaning. I stared at Fin, filled with the wonder of what had happened. He cocked his head, wings neatly tucked now, calm and superior. "Is it true, Fin? Are the ships real?"

I swear even Tullia would have heard the exasperation in his reply. He clacked his beak, rattled deep in his throat, and I translated: Stupid girl. Why else would I waste the effort?

He spread his wings and flapped off toward the fort. I followed at a run.

$$\equiv$$

The ships carried long-awaited friends: Conall Cearnach and two allies from over the sea—Olaib of Norway and Baire of the Scigger Islands. Thanks to my warning, my father was waiting on Baile's Strand to give them welcome. We watched the great ships, stripped now of their billowing sails, anchor in the bay; they hunkered down in the water like broody hens over their nests. The men—hundreds of them—rowed to shore packed into little boats that they pulled up onto the sand.

Conchobor had summoned them. After three years of peace, he had suddenly decided that the insult of Maeve's invasion had not been sufficiently avenged, and that Ulster must have further satisfaction. For although we had prevailed, our brown bull Donn Cooley had been killed in that war. The famed bull's loss must have had gnawed and eaten at Conchobor, at first nothing but a lingering resentment, but growing month by month into a ferocious anger, until he was sick with the need for vengeance.

If anyone questioned the wisdom of Conchobor's campaign, I heard nothing of it. We are a people easily inflamed, and to our warriors, honor and vengeance might as well be the same word.

The narrow strip of beach beyond the reach of high tide was crusted with tents and men and campfires like a layer of barnacles. The men waited for Conchobor's forces to join them en route to Connaught, and for several nights our hall was filled with guests who came to eat and stayed drinking until nearly morning.

I was not allowed to go down to the strand. My mother mistrusted the Norwegians and warned me to stay away from them. "They are rough men," she said darkly, "and no one to know what they might do."

Naturally I snuck off to spy on them. It was easy to stay hidden and unnoticed. But there was nothing I could see that distinguished the foreigners from our own men, who spent their days sleeping and brawling and drinking in more or less equal measures.

☰

Conchobor was well pleased with his raid. They struck at Rosnaree, and Conall Cearnach and my father together could not be withstood.

Strange to say, we at Dun Dealgan were hardly touched by these goings-on. Quite different, it is, when you are not on the receiving end of a raid! My mother was well used to my father being away on his quests and adventures and battles, and she saw to it that our lives continued in their daily pattern. Cuchulainn returned to the same orderly household and well-tended lands he had left, to a welcome that was warm but matter-of-fact. In those days, my father's victory in a fight was no more a matter for doubt than the rising and setting of the sun.

Ξ

My first bleeding came in late winter of that year. We'd had snow in the night—real snow, not just a light dusting that melted off by midmorning, but snow that made a white crystal mystery of the world—and I remember it pleased me to have such dramatic weather mark my passage to womanhood. As my mother took away my childish tunics and dressed me in the new adult clothes she had made for this day—a long linen shift, embroidered at the neck and sleeves, covered by a deep blue woolen overmantle striped with red—I felt an unsettling mixture of excitement and regret.

Tullia sat me down and dressed my hair, still damp from the bath, braiding the front sections and tying the rest in curling cloths. When it had dried, and Tullia had released the curls and fussed some more, my mother gave me a polished bronze mirror in which to admire the results.

I had peeked before, of course, in my mother's mirror. I thought I knew how I looked. So I was unprepared for the serious young woman who stared back at me. I had always thought my dark hair unlovely; it was not bronze-gold like my mother's or even the rich auburn of my father's beard, but a deep oak-leaf brown. But now it cascaded down my shoulders in thick luxurious waves, framing my fair skin and blue eyes like a glossy dark sea. I did not live up to my parents' beauty—I had, perhaps, too much of my father's firm jaw and not enough of my mother's dimpled cheek—yet I liked what I saw well enough.

"The finishing touch," said my mother as she fastened a delicate girdle of linked copper and silver leaves around my waist.

I grinned at her. It was my first piece of precious jewelry, and it made me feel more grown-up than all the rest put together.

"There is more," she said. "Some for your coming of age, and some to put away for your marriage portion."

Marriage portion. There was a sobering thought. I had been looking ahead to the spring Beltane fires—my thirteenth birthday—when I would be presented at the coming-of-age ceremony. It would be grand, I thought, to jump the coals with the other girls who were becoming women that year, while the bystanders sang and cheered. It would be grander still to be old enough to be attending the feasts and gatherings. Only I hadn't thought ahead to the next part. Marriage. It is why men bring their daughters to feast-days, to show them off to potential suitors.

"Don't look so gloomy." My mother sat me down beside her. "You needn't worry yourself—we aren't about to marry off a girl who hasn't even lost her milk teeth."

I glowered at that, feeling she was making me into a baby for the sake of the two stubborn dogteeth that remained anchored firmly in my top gums. And that like to set the tone of the year to come, for it seems I spent it seesawing between alarm when I was taken for an adult and indignation when I was not.

CHAPTER 11
THE STRANGER ON THE STRAND

I paid little enough attention to the news of a young stranger landing in our bay. Ordinarily I would have been curious, for we'd had no visitors at all since the ships of the previous summer. But it was the day of Beltane—my coming of age Beltane—and the only response I remember was disappointment that my father would not be there to sing me across the fire.

"If he is only a boy, why can't the other men deal with him?" I pouted. "For that matter, why should he not choose to keep his name to himself? What harm is there in it?"

"It is the king's command that any who land on our shores give an account of themselves," said my mother. "It is little enough to ask of an uninvited guest." She gave my hair a critical once-over, entirely unmoved by my petulance, and nodded approval to the new girl she had hired to attend me. I still had Tullia, of course, "to watch over your proper behavior," as my mother put it, but I loved having a young companion. Roisin was a hard worker and clever with hair, but she was good company too and only a little older than me. I soon came to value her lively spirit more than the work she saved me.

"And," Emer continued, forestalling my next objection, "boy though he be, he has already handily defeated Conall, who is no poor fighter. It's looking for a fight he is, and he will not rest until he gets it."

I shrugged, a childish ungracious gesture. But I soon got over my resentment. My mother would be at the ceremony, and it's a girl's mother, after all, who guides her to womanhood. And excitement, kept to a seemly murmur through the day, was starting to sing loud in my veins. Beltane was my favorite festival. The sun was very low in the sky now. At dusk it would begin.

≡

I went to my coming-of-age ceremony dressed more beautifully than ever before in my life, with real gold at my arm and throat and golden tips to my braids. By the time the sun rose I would have become a woman in the eyes of my people.

The Samhain fire is built always at the top of an open hill, where it will be a beacon visible far and wide. For Beltane we seek out a more sheltered spot, an open clearing skirted by woodland. Fertility celebrations demand more comfort!

This night, though, I would not be among the children playing tag or rolled into a blanket to sleep under the stars, nor among the older lads and lasses flirting in the pole dance or trysting in the woods. For the first time since my naming-day, I would enter the Sacred Grove and keep vigil there until dawn. The other girls and I would return in time to join in singing the Welcome to the Sun, and then we would do the women's shuffle dance around the dying fires, and leap, one by one, over the coals.

The grove was only about a mile from the Beltane grounds, but it could have been a world away. We were a group of nearly fifteen, all of us giggly and high-strung, heady with our new finery and fighting unadmitted nerves about the night to come—yet as we stepped into that grove we fell completely silent.

The clearing was set within a ring of rowan trees, speckled now with their bitter-smelling white blossoms. Torches flared on stands around the lawn, a central fire burned, and two tall cloaked figures, the druid Daigh and his wife, awaited us on the far side. So simple it was, unimpressive really, but the entire space throbbed silently with a power I could sense with each breath and footstep. We walked through the trees and into the presence of the Sacred, and I felt the thrum of it deep in my own body, like the lowest notes of a drum. Nothing in my experience could really compare, but I was reminded of walking into a thick fog. In that blind swirling world, you feel like you are walking into mystery and could as easily find yourself in the land of the Sidhe or someplace utterly unknown, as on your own laneway.

If the grove was more than I could have imagined, it must be said that the teachings were rather less. We were not initiated into mystery so much as instructed, exhaustively, on the many duties of a wife, a mother and a noblewoman. Any girl with a half-decent upbringing had heard most of it before—though the parts about lying with a man certainly caught our attention! By the time Daigh's earnest wife droned to a close, even the charged atmosphere of the grove couldn't relieve my boredom.

The next part of the ceremony, though, was anything but dull. We were stripped of all our fine clothes and jewels, left with only our cloaks (and how glad I was my mother had insisted I take the heavy warm one rather than the prettier summer weight), and led to a deep pool that bubbled up from the secret depths of the earth. One by one we stepped naked into the icy water, sank below its dark surface and emerged gasping with cold. When my turn came I gritted my teeth and rushed in. Whether I truly left my childhood behind in that black water I do not know, but I thought for some time afterward that I must have left behind a layer of skin, for when I clambered out I could not feel my face or feet or hands, and the rest of my body tingled as if pricked by a thousand tiny needles.

When we came back to the grove, our cloaks wrapped tight as cocoons about us, Daigh had built the fire into a high roaring furnace. We were seated around the fire, blessed with a sprig of rowan, and told to spend the rest of the night in silent meditation, preparing ourselves for our lives to come.

I settled myself into my cloak, lifting my face to the heat of the fire, watching the flames. They said girls sometimes saw their future husbands in those flames. I didn't care so much about that—he would be who he would be, whether I saw him or not—but I did want to make something worthwhile of this night.

I was distracted at first. Some of the girls were fidgety and restless, for we were all uncomfortable. The blaze of fire seared us in front, and the cold breath of night chilled backsides already damp from wet hair.

But the power of that place seeped into me, and little by little the shuffling and complaints faded away, and my own body quieted, until there was only the deep silence of the grove and the leap and dance of the flame. I did look ahead to my future, and I thought again on the teachings we had been given. There was a pattern, I saw, beyond the dull string of individual instructions, and the pattern was a lovelier, more inspiring thing than its small homely parts. We all aspired to be women of honor and respect, to be admired and proud of our accomplishments. But such a life doesn't happen just from wishing it. A destination is reached through many small steps, and what our teachers had tried to give us, in their stolid way, was a map to guide us on our journey.

It was beautiful, what I saw now, how all the small gestures and events and words of a person's life created a pattern completely unique and individual, yet interlaced with the pattern of every other person she touches. My mind was filled with a vision of growing, glowing tendrils of unfolding life, and I sat for a long time feeling the thrust of my own existence and resolving to make of it a bright and beautiful thing.

I was so entranced with my little revelation that it took a long time for the other voice, the dark voice, to be heard. So I cannot say that my happiness gradually became uneasiness. It was more like waking from a pleasant dream to find your house on fire. When the clamor of doom became loud enough to shatter my pretty reverie, the black fingers were already scrabbling deep in my guts, digging and tearing. I bent over, retching—but you cannot vomit away knowledge.

It had never come to me like this, so terribly. So strong and frightening it was, I thought it might be myself who was dying.

You cannot read the message on an Ogham stick while you are being beaten with it. It was like that with me—I was too overwhelmed with the pain to understand what it told me. I did not know then how to step back from the dread and search for its cause. So I lay gasping and groaning in the dark, overcome by some horror I could not name.

May all the gods bless him, it was Fintan who released me. I felt him coming to me even before he arrowed into the grove and plummeted right into my arms. I clutched at him and whispered, "Fin, help me."

I did not need the white feather, not in that place. His black eye, gleaming in the firelight, told me everything. He had been to the strand and seen it all...

The boy looks so slight before my father. He is only a gangly youth, not many years older than me. It is shameful, I think, for my father to fight someone who stands so little chance against him. But the boy stands forth, and when they begin to fight, it is astonishing, for his skill at arms is wonderful and Cuchulainn is hard-pressed by him. They fight for a long time, with neither gaining great advantage over the other, until at last they pull out their spears. My father's Gae Bolga has never failed, and I am glad he will prevail—but I am so sad for the boy. Such courage and skill, such a bright spirit, should not be wasted so.

They wind up for the cast, and here is another marvel, for at the last moment the boy's eyes widen, and he checks his throw, and sends his spear spinning wide of the mark. And as the Gae Bolga sinks deep into his side I am weeping, weeping for them both, for I know what the boy has seen. He has seen his own father.

I saw no more, for the frightened girls had finally run to alert Daigh, and whether by incantation or simply shaking me silly I do not know, but he pulled me out of my vision. I blinked up at him through eyes that swam with tears, disoriented and resentful. His druid's eyes took in Fintan, now stationed protectively in my lap, and my own unfocused gaze, and he promptly sent his wife and the other girls to the far side of the fire. Then he eased himself down beside me.

"What did you see, child?"

His voice was gentle and respectful, but underlaid with that quality druids have which compels a response. Though the tears spilled hot down my cheeks, I found my voice and answered his question.

"My brother is dead."

≡

What veil was drawn over my father's eyes, that he did not know his own son when the signs were so plain before him?

He had waited years for this very day, when the child he had left in Queen Aoife's belly should be old enough to cross the sea from Alba and meet his father. But he had not counted, I suppose, on the resentments a woman can nurse in her breast, and on the terrible fruit such long brooding can bear.

He had conquered her when he fought as Scathach's champion, and however the poets dress it up it seems likely to me that it was the point of his sword, not her own desire, that compelled her to lie with him. Later, perhaps, she did come to love him—Cuchulainn was an easy man to love—but that too ended in bitterness, for he left her to return to Ireland and marry my mother. Perhaps he was shocked to find that she harbored such jealousy and hatred toward him; there was, after all, no promise between them and they parted, as he thought, in friendship. He left her a ring, and bade her name their son Conlaoch and to put him under the tutelage of Scathach when he became of an age to bear arms. She was to send him to Ireland when the ring fit his finger, the way Cuchulainn would recognize him by that token. And if he did not care to tell his new bride about the child he had fathered in Alba, he would not be the first man to keep such news to himself.

And so Aoife did all as Cuchulainn charged her, but she added a charge of her own. For she sent her own son against Cuchulainn as a weapon, to bring about his overthrow. And to ensure the weapon

SERC LIBRARY

would find its target she laid three *geasa*, or taboos, upon the boy: never to give way to any living person, but to die sooner than turn back; never to refuse a challenge from any man, even the greatest champion alive; and third, never to reveal his name on any account, even under threat of death.

And if only Cuchulainn had seen the ring in time, as Conlaoch recognized the famous Gae Bolga, things might have come out differently. But a ring is such a small token. Only when Conlaoch lay dying in his arms did my father know his child. The anguish that came over him then, knowing it was his own hand had cut down his only son and that they would never embrace again in this life, was a crueler vengeance than his own death would have been.

I never did leap the coals of the Beltane fire and complete my journey to womanhood. Dawn found me standing on the strand beside my mother. We watched as my father, waist-deep in the ocean, raged and wept and thrashed his sword wildly against the tireless waves. It was a sight to make the sternest heart break, and the pain and pity of it a thing I still cannot bear to recall.

We kept vigil for three days there on the beach with my father's men. There was no approaching him, but we thought at least to keep him from drowning. And when at last he had exhausted his arms, if not his grief, his men waded through the water and brought him safely home.

Our eyes met as he stumbled onto shore, held on each side by one of his captains. I wanted to look away, pretend I hadn't seen, but I couldn't. I was his only living child, and he would not see me flinch from his suffering.

SEPT LIBRARY

His eyes held the same bruised despair I'd seen in Deirdriu's years before. But there was something else, something somehow worse. My father's shoulders were as broad and powerful as before, his cheeks still smooth and unlined—but his eyes had changed. His eyes were old.

CHAPTER 12
THE CHAMPION FALLS

Did Maeve hate my father for humiliating her army? Or perhaps her attack on him was more impersonal, simply a way to strike a great blow against Ulster. What is certain is that she enlisted any who had ever suffered a loss at my father's hands and invaded Muirthemne set on one prize: Cuchulainn's head. And though Conchobor and Cathbad and my mother, and many others who loved my father, tried to keep him out of the battle for just this reason, in the end it was impossible. He was a warrior. He was born to fight.

Ξ

So we were once again fleeing Dun Dealgan. My mother did not protest this time. Not that it was any easier for her to abandon her home, but the command came from Conchobor and she well understood his intention. It was no secret that Maeve's quarry was the mighty Cuchulainn himself, and Conchobor was determined to keep my father out of the conflict. At the first news of invasion, he was ordered to Emain Macha, to take council with Cathbad and Conchobor and the other advisors, and it is with no little reluctance he obeyed. My mother went along as much to ensure my father did not turn back as for fear of the invaders.

It was a more comfortable journey, at least, for I had my own horse now. Orlagh was my pride and joy, a blond beauty with black points and an eager heart. Remembering the long weary

vigil we had kept before at Emain Macha, my mother took
her best maidservant and said that Roisin should come too.
Tullia stayed behind to nurse Eirnin, who was ill with a racking
cough.

Roisin was beside herself with excitement at the prospect of
going to Emain. She was a woman of good rank in her own
right, daughter to one of the smiths who supplied my father's
warriors and of an age to be thinking of marrying. She tried
hard to restrain herself, for the occasion was hardly a happy one,
but she was an adventurous girl who had never been away from
Muirthemne, and here she was heading to the king's own court.
Was there anywhere in Ulster more likely to be well-stocked with
comely young men? I did not begrudge her eagerness, though I
could not share it.

We were in my chamber, sorting through clothes and Roisin
peppering me with questions, when my mother came to me.

"Luaine, leave Roisin to do the packing. I want you to ride out
with me now, before we leave Dun Dealgan."

She would not speak of our errand—not one word—while the
horses were saddled, but set out at a great clip north toward the
Cooley Mountains.

It was nearly summer, a humid warm morning, and by the time
we slowed our horses the sweat was trickling down my back. My
bafflement had turned to hot irritation, and it told in my voice
as I asked again, "Ma, what is this about?"

She half-turned in her saddle to face me. "There is something
I must show you," she said. "And you must pay attention, in case
you ever have need to find this place by yourself."

"You see this low hill before us—it's the first foothill of the

Cooleys." I knew the hill well—had looked out at it from Dun Dealgan every day of my life—but I scanned it now with new interest.

Emer continued. "You see that place where the gorse ends and the forest comes down in a point to meet it?"

I nodded, trying to fix the spot in my memory. "The hill looks like a giant woman lying there," I said, sweeping my hand in an imaginary caress from ankle to shoulder. "The trees are like her belly and the gorse her thigh."

My mother raised an eyebrow at that. "If you say so. But yes, that place. It's only a rough landmark, for the vegetation pattern will change year by year. But we start by making for the tip of that line of trees."

We rode on, much slower once we reached the hill and found the narrow path that threaded its way between trees and head-high thickets of gorse, its flowers so intensely yellow when the sun caught them they almost hurt my eyes. As we rode, my mother told me at last what we were there for.

My parents had realized early on that a border fort like Dun Dealgan was vulnerable to sudden raids, and they had made a cache for their accumulated wealth. There were two such caches now, about a half-mile apart, and my mother took me to both, pointing out in each case the landmarks that would lead me there and the inconspicuous but unmistakable marker that pointed to the exact spot.

"The wealth we have at Dun Dealgan is only a portion of the war-prizes and rewards your father has claimed," Emer explained to me. "Even if Dun Dealgan is burned to the ground and every goblet looted, what we have hidden away here is enough to start again. There is a bride-portion for you here, and more. Do you understand me?" And her green eyes searched mine, luminous with a message of their own.

"Yes, Ma, I understand." I didn't though, not completely. Not until later. My mind was busy memorizing locations, and marveling at this sudden revelation of riches, and worrying about the threat to my father. I was too preoccupied to hear what was between my mother's words.

Ξ

My father knew well enough that death awaited him on our own plain of Muirthemne. There were omens and portents enough to write doom for any fool, and Cathbad's warnings as well. Of course a champion will seek a great name, even to his downfall. But I do not believe it was a warrior's bravado that made my father shake off our restraining hands. When he said to Cathbad, "I am glad and ready enough to go into the fight, though I know as well as you yourself I must fall in it," I believe he spoke simple truth.

He had given his life to the warrior's code, you see, to a dream of glory and honor and high deeds. But when Conlaoch died, the very foundations of that life were shattered. What was honor, or the truth of a warrior's word, or great feats of arms—what were any of them worth, if what they led to was shame and horror? He had killed the boy he longed to love, the son he dreamed of, the one who should have been fighting at his side.

He was glad to go down fighting. Better the sword and the spear and the next life to come, than to carry such pain.

It is no honor to the tribes of Ireland, though, the way they killed my father. The poets are respected for their great learning, and this is why no one should lightly refuse to grant a boon to them. And yes, perhaps they are feared a little too, for their satires bring dishonorable acts to light, and can bring down the highest leader. But it is Maeve used her poets for blackmail and deceit. And I myself have seen how this corruption has spread, and tasted its black fruits.

So she set her three poets against Cuchulainn in the battle. Each called out and asked for a boon, and each time the boon requested was his spear. For it was foretold that only Cuchulainn's own spear could kill him. And they threatened to put a bad name on him and on his kin if he refused. And my father, knowing that death was on him, would not have his name sullied in any way, and so he gave up his spears—making sure each one found its mark in its new owner's head as he threw it.

Those spears were given to Maeve's greatest warriors. One killed Laeg, who had never wavered from my father's side. The second pierced The Gray, a king among horses. The third, thrown by Lughaid, gave my father a deadly wound.

Still his enemies feared to come near him. My father was unhindered as he took his belt and bound himself to the tall pillar-stone that thrust like a giant's finger out of the battlefield, the way he would die standing on his feet, a proud warrior to the end. And the men of Ireland circled around, but did not dare approach until the hero-light faded from Cuchulainn's face and they were sure he was dead. They say that the Morrigu's crow of death came and settled on Cuchulainn's shoulder as he stood tied to his pillar, and that he gave a great laugh when he saw it, in defiance of death itself.

Crow, indeed.

That was my Fintan, sent to watch over my father and to bring word of the outcome to my mother and me, where we waited in Emain Macha. And the one small comfort I gain from this whole sad tale is that my father laughed at the sight of him. He recognized Fin. And if he recognized him, it may be he understood the message of love Fintan carried, from my heart to his.

CHAPTER 13
EMER'S GRIEF

I had never known my mother to act the way she did in Emain Macha, as we waited for news of my father. Silent, still and distant she was—so far from the bustling outspoken woman I had grown up with that I barely recognized her. Her entire mind and heart were given over to the waiting, and she spent most of every day on the ramparts gazing south. I trailed in her wake, watching over the watcher.

We were seated there together when Fintan returned to me. We watched his heavy wingbeats flap across the fields, my mother in a sudden agony of anxiety.

"What does he say?"

Fintan had barely landed when my mother's urgent question prodded me into action. For my part, I was suddenly reluctant to ask. Fintan's visions are not always easy to see, and the darkness that had been growing in my own heart was squeezing at it cruelly now. I knew, with sick certainty, what was to come.

But the sight of it—it doesn't matter what omens or forebodings come before, nothing can prepare a person to witness a loved one's death. To see my father sagging against the Old Ones' stone, his guts spilling from his body, his enemies circling like a pack of wolves...it was unbearable. When Lughaid's sword swept off his head I cried out against it as though I stood there beside him, and the shrill sound of my own voice wrenched me from the bloody scene.

"What?" my mother demanded. She shook me, heedless of my sobs. "What is it?"

"He is dead, Ma." I choked out the words, unable to stop crying. I thought I had been prepared for his death—we all knew this was his most perilous challenge, and knew too the prophecy foretelling his early end—but watching it had made it too real, too brutal. The image of him tied there, with The Gray slipping in his own blood but defending my father with teeth and hooves to the last, burned behind my eyes. I was overcome with pity, with pride in their courage, with my own loss.

I reached out to my mother, thinking to comfort each other, and was met with a resounding slap that all but knocked me down. I stared at her, shocked beyond words, my stinging cheek unheeded.

Her eyes sparked like green fire. She hissed at me, a wildcat in human form. "How dare you speak such lies to me! You and that black apparition! You would have me give up hope on the say-so of some carrion crow? And you but an untrained girl!"

She turned her back on me, returning her gaze to the gentle roll of the hills. "My faith is with Cuchulainn," she snapped. "And I will not break it."

Hot indignation rose in me at the injustice of it. It was my mother who had urged me to send Fintan, and now…

It is as well I was beyond speech then, for whatever I might have said I would regret now. Instead I watched her, and slowly I began to feel the effort of will that straightened my mother's back and firmed her trembling lip. The will that would hold onto hope until its last shred crumbled to dust and seeped from her grasp.

Fintan and I had been close for years. Experience had taught me to trust his messages. But my mother? I saw now that my news had frayed what little hope was left to her, without giving her the certainty that would allow her to let it go. I wished now I had found a way to keep Fin's news to myself.

I left my mother then and ran to my chamber, so as not to hurt her more with my tears. I curled up like a wounded animal and wept, not for the great champion of Ulster, but for the man who sliced apples with his sword, took a small girl flying across the plains, and laughed with a sound like chimes.

☰

I was but a young child when I first saw trophy heads hanging from my father's girdle, swinging in gory counterpoint to his stride. The House of the Red Branch in Emain was festooned with them, and they gave me little pause. I had never questioned our practice of taking enemy heads.

The day my father came home without his, I felt differently. They tried to lay him out with dignity, there on the lawns before the Speckled House, but for all their drums and weeping and reverence, they could not change brute reality. The fact is, a man without his head hardly seems human at all.

He looked like a butchered animal, lying there. He had gone to his last battle in the old style he preferred, naked but for his weapons harness and his gold. His fair skin had been bled white as marble and blotched with bruising; his limbs had stiffened so that he did not rest on the ground but lay braced against it. A bloody cloth wound about his belly, holding together the mess that lay beneath. I tried, the gods know I tried, to see my father in that body, but I could not seem to see beyond the dark crusted stump of his neck.

I turned away, trying to stifle the groan of revulsion that escaped my throat.

My mother, though. My mother never flinched from Cuchulainn's ravaged body. She stood full of calm dignity, now that all guessing and hope were past, and her eyes caressed his poor limbs as though she saw no horror, but only her own beloved. They were dark with sorrow and luminous with love, unmarred by tears.

"Bring water, and his best cloak." Emer's maid, Osnait, hovered at her elbow, sobbing convulsively. I could see that only her duty to my mother kept her from giving way altogether and throwing herself to the ground. All around us people wailed and sobbed and tore at their hair—a seductive hysteria that pulled at me as well. You can lose yourself in a great outpouring of grief, so that it becomes a kind of shelter. But my mother's curt command pulled Osnait back from the brink, and after one last, wild-eyed look at my father's body, she hurried into the great house.

Emer washed him as tenderly as a baby, right there in front of Conchobor's household, and we might as well have been wisps of mist for all she minded us. Even when I knelt beside her and tried to help, she said nothing, but brushed me off as absently as if I were one of the flies that feasted on my father's wounds.

I stood at the edge of the solitude my mother had created for herself, and the fist around my heart squeezed with such a complexity of pain that I could not pull breath into my lungs. Grief for my father's death was almost eclipsed by the awful sight of Emer struggling to wrap my father in his cloak with his weaponry. It was not a job for one person, but she snarled at the warrior who bent to help her lift up Cuchulainn's body, and he withdrew instantly. Cuchulainn had been Ulster's darling in life, but in death my mother claimed him as hers alone. There was no one else in the world for her at that moment, and that knowledge filled me with pity.

And yes, I was angry at her too, though it was years before I could admit it even to myself. She pushed me away in her grief, and it was the hurt and loneliness of it—that she had no thought to spare for her living child, but only for her dead husband—that sucked the very air away from me.

I was actually bent over, gasping for breath and fighting back the black dots that danced before my eyes, when I heard a commotion behind me. There was jostling and muttering, and finally a clear voice broke through. "Make way, for pity's sake, or I swear I will kick you from my path!"

It was Roisin, and I have never been so glad to hear sauce from an underling. I had given her a free day rather than have her sit around watching me wait with my mother. But when the news reached her, she came running. Her strong young arms wrapped around me from behind, her voice murmured in my ear, and finally the knot in my windpipe loosened. I straightened up with a deep breath that released with a racking sob, turned into the warmth of her breast, and wept against her.

A stir rustled through the crowd, and Roisin's voice identified its cause. "A rider, Luaine. A warrior."

In full battle gear he was, his horse streaked with sweat and foamy in the mouth from hard riding. He pulled up hard, dismounted, strode straight to my mother, and knelt in deference.

My mother was fussing with a brooch, working to fasten the cloak smooth and tight with the brooch perfectly placed,

oblivious to the grisly stump it adorned. I could tell the warrior, war-hardened as he was, was discomfited by this homely
tenderness. He cast his eyes to the ground and waited for her
acknowledgment.

He waited a long time, while my mother ignored him utterly.
I was appalled to find myself amused at his nervous glances, the
war between impatience and hesitation that played out on his
features. What kind of unfeeling daughter could I be? But it is
the way our human heart is made, the laughter and the tears
lying so close together that they sometimes blend into each other
against our will.

Finally the messenger steeled himself to reach out and touch
her shoulder.

"Lady Emer."

Her head snapped up, and I wondered if she would strike him,
but he hurried on and the words he spoke were enough to earn
her attention:

"I bear a message from Conall Cearnach, who bids you not
put Cuchulainn into his grave until he returns to you. For he has
sworn to avenge the death of his dear foster-son, and it is your
husband's head he will return with, and the head of Lughaid who
took it from him, and heads from every tribe of Ireland besides,
until the men of Munster and Connaught and Leinster will be
crying for the rising they made against him."

My mother stood then, so regal in her bearing, and lifted the
messenger also to his feet.

"Tell Conall we will wait," she said gravely. "For it is good there
is one still in Ulster with the courage to bring home what is due
to me now, and to my lord's memory."

And she sent him off, without so much as a fresh horse or a drink of water.

Ξ

So we were once again in the Speckled House, my father laid out with candles all about him, my mother keeping vigil and drifting ever deeper into a world apart.

I do not mean to say she was mad. People came by to pay their respects, and she received them graciously. She discussed plans for the burial rites with Conchobor, and I do not believe he noticed anything amiss—unless that she was remarkably composed.

But Osnait and I, who knew her well, we noticed. She was not mad—she was *absent*. Her eyes looked through us, never making real contact. She did not refuse the broth and tidbits of food Osnait pressed on her, or the sleeping draughts from Cathbad; she accepted them with thanks and left everything untouched. For three days and nights, she did not eat, did not sleep, did not bathe or change her clothes or arrange her hair or speak one word of what was in her heart. And gradually my worry for her turned to a whispery cold fear.

"Why does she not weep?" I demanded of Roisin. I sat up in my bed, unable to sleep for the crawling anxiety in my gut. "She holds in her grief. She allows no one to hold or comfort her." Not even me, the bitter thought followed unbidden.

It was not a thing I was used to. We are hardly a people to hide our feelings. It did not frighten me to see a grown man roar with anger, or a woman fall down shrieking with grief. But this…this made the black fist writhe in my belly.

"I don't know, Mistress." Roisin's voice was reassuringly real in the dark. I heard the whisper of her blankets and then the rustle of straw as her weight settled beside me. She rarely called me "Mistress" anymore, except in public. Roisin was a woman with a natural gift for helping and an aversion to serving, and she was too close to the sister I never had for me to want to change her. Tonight, though, hearing my title bolstered me. She was reminding me of who I was, and the strength that should match my position.

We sat in silence, and I let the warm relaxed weight of her arm across my shoulders seep down and settle my jumpy nerves. I was feeling that I might sleep, after all, when she spoke again.

"I have seen something like it in an animal, I think." Her voice was tentative, fearing perhaps to give offense. I kept silent, inviting her to continue.

"It was a pair of hounds we had, reared from pups together. They were old—maybe close to ten years—when the bitch died. And the dog acted so strange. He guarded her body, would let no one near it without growling. My pa was going to kick him off, but my ma said to let him be. And the next morning he let us bury her."

I thought about her story, trying to find the window into my mother's heart. There was a similarity, but was there a meaning?

"Maybe your ma is not ready to let go of him," Roisin suggested. "Maybe she is saving her grief for the burial rites."

She had not studied with druids and poets, but Roisin was wise in understanding nonetheless.

Ξ

I could take no satisfaction in the heads Conall presented to us. He laid them out in rows on the lawn, grisly fruits in a warrior's garden. More death, more butchered bodies sent home to their families, more vengeance to be exacted. Will there be a warrior left standing, I wondered wearily, when all accounts are paid? But my mother praised Conall for his courage and loyalty and prowess, and listened rapt to the account of his one-handed duel with Lughaid, and to see her face alert and interested again gave me hope.

Finally he laid in her arms a bundle, apologizing for the rough wrapping. Cuchulainn's head. My own tears welled up as Emer cradled and stroked it, and I came forward, longing suddenly to see him, touch him even, however disfigured the poor face. The memory of him swept over me so clearly then: his long easy stride, the sparkle of his eyes, the strong circle of his arms, the way the sun brought out all the colors in his hair. I could not let him go to the ground without even looking upon his end.

But my mother stood suddenly and called Osnait to her, and they hurried off to the great house. And there she did all that the poets recount: bathed Cuchulainn's head and combed out the bright hair; wrapped it in rich silk as green as the barley fields in spring. But she did it alone, locked into the room we had once shared, and she did not come out until it was time for my father's last farewell and all but her gathered at the graveside, waiting.

She was transformed, her hair arrayed in shining braids and loops, her dress immaculate, the gold gleaming at her throat and arm and waist. She was beautiful beyond words, like a queen of the Sidhe, and she bore her burden of green silk as if it were a crown for a king.

But as she approached, the dark fingers clawed and clutched in my guts and my mouth filled with the taste of fear. I looked to Cathbad, somber in his splendid robe, and found only dark sorrow in the eyes that followed Emer's journey. Perhaps that was all I felt as well—the full fierce grasp of grief. And why not? All around me, men and women wept openly for my father.

My mother gave no sign that she noticed anyone or anything but the body that lay on its burial board, surrounded by weapons and riches, and the head that lay heavy in her hands. The emerald eyes that had once flashed with wit and pride were soft and lost and blind. I understood then that she had not dressed for a public appearance. She had dressed for her lover alone.

She laid my father's head against his body in regal silence. And then, at last, she fell upon him and gave way to weeping. And the lament she spoke for him as they lowered him into the grave was as beautiful and spirited as Emer herself.

But I could not listen. I could hardly hear her words, so loud did the fear clamor in my head, so black was the darkness that filled me. If Roisin's hand had not held firm to my girdle, I could not have stayed up on my own legs.

My mother pulled herself away and stood silent as they lowered my father's body. And then it happened. As he came to rest at the bottom of the grave, she leapt down to him. The bright knife flashed in her hand. Red blood spilled from her throat as she fell.

I watched my mother take her own life and die with the man she loved. And all I could think at first, through the shock and my own horror, was that she had cast me away on the winds of the world.

CHAPTER 14
LOST ON THE WIND

And so I was carried along, aimless as thistle fluff. I remember only snatches of the days following my mother's death, for they rolled past like thick gray fog. I could not bear to think about what had happened, and so I could not think about anything at all. And Cathbad must have thought I needed this respite, for he plied me with brews that wrapped me in blurry warmth and made me sleep for hours on end.

It was Roisin who coaxed me back to myself. She tended me like a baby when I could do nothing on my own, and gradually her easy talk while she spooned soup into me or brushed my hair began to reach me. I remember my first painful awakening. Roisin was describing a litter of pups that had been born to a young man she had taken a liking to. "So funny they are, with their big milk bellies and crybaby complaints and the way they burrow and squirm to get the best teat. He says he will give me my pick of them, and I have set my heart on one with a coal black coat and a long white blaze up his muzzle."

That stirred something in me. I straightened in my chair, forced my eyes to focus until I found Roisin's brown eyes, bright with sympathy, fixed on my own.

"Where is Fintan?" I asked.

Ξ

"It is a fine young woman you have become, Luaine, and I want you to know I will help you in any way that I can."

The king's heavy hand covered mine protectively. I tried hard to follow Conchobor's words. My mind was clearer now, and I had stopped taking Cathbad's numbing drinks, but I still found it so hard to sustain a train of thought—especially if it had to do with my life or future. I could not seem to believe in a future.

"My thanks, Sire. I am grateful for your concern." My mouth spoke the required words, while my thoughts looped away. The king had asked to see me in his private hall, and Roisin had fussed over my hair and dress as if I was off to a feast.

"Roisin, really. He will just be giving his condolences."

"He is the king," she insisted stubbornly. "And you will need him on your side."

There it was—the future again. What was I to do, once I had done hiding in my chamber in Emain Macha? My father had no brothers, no sons, to share ownership of his lands. His own father, Sualtim, was dead. So Muirthemne and Dun Dealgan itself were mine. But could I maintain them? I was ready to run a household, no doubt, but Dun Dealgan was a border outpost. How could a fourteen-year-old girl command a garrison army?

"Don't be silly," Roisin had chided. "Look at you. You are young and lovely, noble of birth, wealthy, educated. You are the daughter of the first man and woman of Ulster. You will have your pick of fine champions eager to share your marriage bed and defend your lands."

I supposed she was right. I didn't know, exactly, how to look for a husband, and could not summon much enthusiasm at the prospect. Perhaps in time my path would be plainer.

"Your father, my sister's son, was very dear to me, and I feel I owe it to him to ensure his child has every protection." Conchobor's deep voice droned on. He was stroking my hand, and he had pulled his chair close to mine. I could feel the heat of his leg against my own. I had never been so close to the king, and I saw now the age behind his fine jewels and fabrics. His cheeks were traced with purple veins, his fingernails thickened and yellow. His teeth would not be long in his head from the look of them. I nodded politely.

"You are very kind."

"You have considerable holdings, you know, Luaine. Lands. The fort itself. Herds, and your father's bondsmen and his warriors. It's a heavy responsibility for a young girl. And you are vulnerable, in your grief and your youth. The greedy, the unscrupulous—all will have an eye to your wealth. I fear you may find yourself under attack all too soon."

This was more than condolences. I told myself to take hold of my thoughts, to pay attention. After all, this was Conchobor's concern as well. If Muirthemne fell, it would be territory lost to Ulster.

"I understand, Sire. I have had these thoughts myself," I replied. I glanced at his face, found him nodding enthusiastically. He could help me, I realized, by taking on the role my family might have played. He *was* my family, after all. I took a deep breath. "I have been advised," I said cautiously, "to marry a man who can take over the defense of the Muirthemne plain." I had dreamed, of course, of a great love match. The dream, buried under layers of grief as it was, fluttered in protest. But my mother's passion had ended in ashes. I wrapped myself in indifference, and the gossamer wings stilled.

The king's thick fingers tightened over mine, and he smiled at me approvingly. "That was my exact thought, Luaine. A match that will secure your lands and guarantee you the safety and comfort you deserve." He would help, then. Hope, or maybe just relief, rose within me. With the king himself to consider potential suitors and negotiate on my behalf, life began to seem possible. Conchobor's voice rumbled on, something about my fine looks and noble upbringing, but my thoughts had turned again to my mother's fall, the way her skirts had billowed up in the wind and the first terrifying spurt of blood from her neck...

"...So you see, you need have no more worries. You have the love and protection of the king now and will want for nothing. Emain Macha has been too long without a queen."

Lugh help me, what had he said? My mind scrambled to reconstruct the stream of words while I gawped at him like a fool.

"That's right, my dear." Did I imagine it? The smile was gentle and indulgent, but a cutting edge of will held it in place. "I will wed you myself. I care that much for your welfare. You shall be my queen."

I cast my eyes down, coloring in confusion, as he underlined his claim by sliding his arm behind my waist, pulling me close, and pressing his lips into the hollow of my neck.

"The sooner, the better, I think," he said briskly. "No sense in leaving matters unsettled."

He was King, he was telling me. He would wed whom—and when—he would.

Ξ

"Well?" Roisin was not about to let me sink back into my fog.

"I am to wed the king," I said weakly.

There was a long silence, and I knew without looking that Roisin was struggling to master her dismay. King or not, he would not have been her choice. Nor mine, not that it made any difference.

Bless her, she did not repeat the obvious: that Conchobor was four times my own age, that I had had no chance to mourn my parents or recover from their loss, that I might prefer to stay in my own home. Instead she found the only words left to say.

"You will be queen, Luaine—queen of all Ulster! First among all the women!" She came over to me and took my hands and kissed them, her face solemn now. "Be happy, my lady. You deserve it."

I managed a smile—a little shaky, but genuine. And then I saw, as if in a waking dream, Roisin's sharp features blur into bruised violet eyes and corn silk hair. Just for a moment, Deirdriu's pale face floated before me. I watched it fade into shadow—and I burst into tears.

≡

My parents were hardly a week in the ground when I found myself sitting beside King Conchobor, in the place where I had first seen Deirdriu, at my betrothal feast.

Everything was happening so fast, I could not keep up with my own life. I had been moved into a large luxurious room and surrounded by a flurry of women armed with fabric samples and jewelry, taking my measurements, buffing my nails, scenting my bathwater. Messengers had been sent to Dun Dealgan, telling my father's men they were now in direct service to the king and to hold the territory in readiness for a new warlord. And in the midst of this confusion came a visit from Cathbad himself.

He took me away from the bustle, to his own quiet dark house. Fintan was there, and I was stricken to think how I had ignored him these long days.

"Fintan is fine," Cathbad said quietly. "It is you I am concerned with."

He left me alone to visit with Fin, and slowly the silence and privacy seeped down into my soul and loosened the great knot of grief I had locked away there. I found myself weeping, my tears dripping and beading up on Fintan's feathers, and I did not try to stay them but let them pour freely until at last the great rushing sobs quieted and then stilled. It was the first time I was able to truly feel what had happened to me, and the tears brought release and healing and the return of my own strength.

I don't know how long Cathbad left me there, in the one place in all of Emain Macha sure to be free from intrusion. When he returned, he took my face in his hands and stared down into my eyes.

"Better," he nodded.

"I should think they would look worse," I ventured.

"Red as a drunkard's," he agreed. "But better for all that."

He sat down beside me, the dark penetrating gaze searching me still as I stroked Fintan and tried not to squirm.

"And now I must ask you something, Luaine, for Conchobor has asked me to announce your betrothal and to set the bride-price on your behalf. And while I serve the king, I serve the gods and the law also. And so I would know: do you agree to this match?"

I had never really asked myself the question. Now, in the quiet place Cathbad had made for me, I searched for my own will.

I had no love for the king. I could not imagine the king's marriage bed would be a shared pleasure. So there was regret there, that I would not have a man I could delight in, when I had never even lain with a boy my own age.

But I had known enough real tragedy to realize that this was no tragedy. I was not Deirdriu, pining for her true love. My father had served the king, and Conchobor had been generous and loyal in return. He offered me a place of honor before the women of Ulster. My sons would be high princes. My daughters would stand tall in the eyes of our people.

I did not pretend to myself that I could refuse the offer. The choice was in my own heart: to submit unwillingly or to take my place as a true queen.

"Yes," I told Cathbad, "I agree to the match."

CHAPTER 15
THE POET'S CURSE

Shame, Blemish and Disgrace. That is what they call the three blisters raised by a poet's curse, the blemishes that kill. But it is not to myself the shame and the disgrace belong. It is to Aithirne's sons, who tarnished the poet's calling and betrayed their honor.

I had been married less than a month when Conchobor took Cathbad and his other advisors, along with a troop of men, to Tara, the sacred center of Ireland. Maeve and Ailill had proposed a meeting, to exchange sureties of peace on either side. Conall Cearnach's revenge had told on them, I suppose. I confess I was glad to see the king off; I was doing my best to play the proud young queen, but it was a lot to get used to. For a start, I had a hard time sleeping with a heavy snoring man pressed against me, and the thought of a few nights with a bed to myself were cheering.

The first day I slept, and then I wandered about with Roisin and allowed myself to be a girl again. On the second day, I decided it was time to visit my parents' grave.

I dressed, not in my new finery, but in clothes I had brought from Dun Dealgan, wanting to come to them as the girl they had known. I put on the girdle of interlocking leaves my mother had given me in my first womanhood, and then I strapped on the sword that was my father's gift. I come to honor you both, I thought.

And I came alone, despite the protests of the flock of women who attended me. I drew myself up to my full height—I was as tall as my mother now and growing still. I tried to feel within me the authority Emer had worn so easily and searched within myself for a voice belonging to a queen, not a rebellious girl.

"This is a private matter," I said. "I would be alone with my parents, this last time, and have a space to grieve undisturbed." And just like that, the nattering and scolding stopped, and they nodded respectfully and drew back. All except Roisin, who flashed me a cheeky grin and gave her fist a discreet twitch that eloquently cheered my success as she drifted out with the others.

It was a beautiful early autumn day, the light achingly clear, the fields turning golden, the air fragrant with harvest. The orchards would be heavy with fruit. The clouds passed high overhead, fleeting shadows with no threat of rain. It was a day to make even a graveyard beautiful.

They had put one great stone over the grave, engraved along two edges with Ogham. I knelt before it, and with my fingers I traced first one line—Cuchulainn, son of Sualtim—and then the other—Emer, daughter of Forgall. Two names, nothing more.

"Raise my stone over the grave of the Hound," I murmured, "since it is through my grief for him I go to my death." The last words I heard my mother say.

"It has been done, Ma," I said to the blue sky. "May you be happy together, in whatever your next life holds."

≡

Only the kings of Ulster are buried within the walls of Emain Macha. The burial ground where my parents rested lay west of the walls, for it is beyond the setting sun the souls of the dead must journey.

I took the long way back to the gate, leaving the road to walk through the orchards. It was the closest I had been to happiness in months, rambling under the fragrant trees with only Fintan and my own thoughts for companions.

"If only we could smell the sea, Fin." I had a powerful longing, suddenly, for our quiet days in Muirthemne, the sweet roll of the plain falling away on every side and always, to the east, the endless expanse of the sea. My life now seemed to plunge along without me, and there was no going back to the child I once was.

I had realized almost immediately that Conchobor was not looking for a real queen, or even a real wife, but only an ornament for his arm. I wondered if even his first wife, the mother of his grown sons, had played any role in the governing of his kingdom before she died. If so, he had since grown used to ruling alone, relying on his trusted advisors. He was not about to include a mere girl, inexperienced and untried. For that matter, why should he?

So I would not be a powerful queen. But I should at least be head of my own household. Yet how was I to manage a house that had run on its own, under the iron hand of the steward, for so many long years? I was sure Deirdriu had not even tried. When I walked into the kitchens or asked to see the storerooms I was made to feel an intruder, despite the surface deference. There was nothing for me to do but dress my hair, try on the jewels Conchobor gave me, pretend that my needlework was more than a way to pass the time, and be a gracious conversationalist at table until the men were too drunk to notice. Even in private, Conchobor paid me little mind. He had done nothing but snore and fart in our marriage bed since the quick drunken coupling of our wedding night. Not that I had any desire for him—far from it—but it was a humiliation that he had so little desire for me.

The golden sun and sweet silence washed over me as I walked along, puzzling over what I had become. Was this what my parents would have wished for me? From the outside, it seemed the very pinnacle of what I had been trained for. But the reality of it felt wrong.

Fintan's raucous call, some way ahead, jarred me from my reverie. I wondered what—or who—he had found. A few minutes later, as I left the last of the trees behind and returned to the broad road that skirted the walls of Emain Macha, I saw walking toward me the two men who had attracted Fin's attention. Redheaded, as like as twins, they were easy to recognize: Aithirne's sons, Cuingedach and Abhartach. They were poets, like their father, and they had said high words at my wedding in praise of Conchobor and of myself.

I smiled and nodded a greeting to them as they approached, then I stopped in surprise as each man sank to one knee before me. As queen I would expect a respectful greeting, but the noblemen I knew were not over-fond of kneeling.

"It is our fair young queen!" proclaimed one. Cuingedach or Abhartach? I had not yet learned to tell them apart. "Luaine of the curly locks. Luaine with eyes as deep and blue as the sea. Luaine of the white throat, more beautiful than any torque or jewel that could adorn it."

I had to grin. I supposed I would get used to it in time, but except for my wedding—when, after all, they were required to find something nice to say—I had never been the subject of a poet's praise. The giddy pleasure of it made my cheeks flush, and I had a bit of a struggle to regain my sense of decorum and give a suitably dignified reply.

"I thank you for your kind words." I made to walk on, but the other one reached out for my hand.

"A boon, my lady. A boon for me and my brother."

Sudden caution rumbled in my belly. I was a queen now, I reminded myself. It was a privilege and duty of my position to be hospitable and generous, and a mark of my standing that I could be asked a gift. I should be proud of the request—I *was* proud of the request. But the story of my father's death had revealed to me the menace that can lie behind a poet's words. I took a step backward.

"What boon would you request?" And though I tried to keep my voice calm and regal, I could hear the fear in it.

Suddenly they were both standing, pressing me on either side, their voices, so similar, a confused intermingling in my ears.

"We are suffering, Luaine, suffering from our love for you."

"From the first day we looked upon you, our desire has grown."

"It is a fire within us, my lady. It scorches and withers us. It is dead we will be, burned away by love, if you do not save us."

"We are desperate before your beauty. Have mercy on our need, we beg of you."

I could not believe what I was hearing, and my very incredulity left no room for fear. I pushed them both away from me.

"Are you mad? I am your king's wife. You heard me take my marriage vows. I will not dishonor his name, nor my word!"

Their faces darkened, and the realization came upon me that I could be in real danger. One does not anger a poet lightly. I tried to soften my voice.

"Ask of me another boon, an honorable boon, I pray you. If it is within my power to grant it, I will."

Four pale eyes stared at me, and I saw within them no fire of love, but rather cold will. And then they were on me, dragging me back into the orchard, pinning me against a tree, pressing themselves against me, and all the while one hand was clamped across my mouth so I could barely draw breath, and other hands pulled at my clothing and clutched at my body, and their voices hissed at me:

"We will quench our fires within you, whether you will or not."

"You must be a friend to poets, little queen. Those who are not are soon sorry."

I struggled against them, but there seemed no way to get an arm or leg free from their clutches, and in the next instant I was pushed to my knees.

There was an explosion in the trees, an ear-splitting screech. Fintan crashed into one brother's head, claws outstretched, wings pummeling. Whoever it was he hit cried out and staggered back, beating uselessly at the unseen foe behind him.

It was all I needed. The red rage flowered within me, a heat that burned through my limbs and flamed behind my eyes. I was on my feet, my knee snapping up with a force I didn't know I had, square between my remaining assailant's legs. I had my sword free of its scabbard in time to meet his throat as he doubled over. And this time the voice that spoke held no hint of fear, but rang out clear and confident.

"I have not yet blooded this sword, but you can be sure I know how. Do not think the Hound has left his daughter unable to defend herself. It is only respect for your station that keeps me from slitting your throat.

"Get away from me now, and do not come near to me again, or Conchobor will hear of your shameful acts. And know that I will be girded with this sword from now on, and that next time I will not hesitate to use it."

Fintan flapped over and perched protectively on my shoulder. The man I had kicked stumbled backward, still bent over, his face drained of all color from the pain. His brother, though, was scarlet with anger.

"You think it so simple a matter, to spurn a poet? You think a sword will protect you?"

"I think I have heard enough of your poison tongue. Take your brother and leave my sight."

He turned his back to me, helping his brother regain his feet. I kept my sword leveled against them. And then, in a single swift motion, he twirled and flicked his arm.

Pain seared into my face. I cried out, clapping one hand to my cheek. A sharp shard was embedded there, the pain of it like a hundred hornet stings. Hot blood spilled through my fingers as the fiery needles pierced deeper with each beat of my pulse.

Laughter, scornful and triumphant, rang in my ears. I raised my sword once more.

"Poison tongue indeed, little slut! You will see now what the ill will of the poets can do. Your name will be reviled throughout Ulster as the most faithless of wives. And you—you, Luaine, daughter of the mighty Cuchulainn though you be—you will die."

I watched in horror, through a haze of pain, as Abhartach took up the position of the spellcaster: balanced on one leg, one arm extended so that the finger pointed straight toward me, he glared at me through one eye and hurled the words of power in a voice that carried to the skies. "I, Abhartach Mac Aithirne, curse you. Let Shame, Blemish and Disgrace rise upon your face for all to see, and let them spread, and eat away your heart, and kill you."

CHAPTER 16
THE DANCE OF DEATH

The strength drained from my legs like the receding tide and they buckled of their own accord and without my notice. What gripped me, I know now, was fear, but I thought at the time I would die right there under the trees. My vision had darkened and blurred, so that I looked down a kind of hazy tunnel to see only the two brothers as they swaggered down the road. There was a drumming in my ears that drowned out thought, the violent blows of a heart that seemed to have swelled up into my throat and must soon burst from its casing or crush my windpipe.

Cursed is what that drumming said. *You are cursed, cursed, cursed...*

I had been raised to venerate the poets. My models were men like my teacher Lasair, a man of learning who delighted in his own words, yet was patient with a child's imperfect efforts to recite them. Men like Sencha, Conchobor's peacemaker, a man respected by all for his wise words and fair mind. Abhartach and Cuingedach were of another type entirely. I had not dreamed of such treachery and malice.

I was cursed, and I would die. Seven days it takes, for the poet's curse to bring its victim to death. My name would be tainted with their evil lies, Cuchulainn's line ended in shame.

Ξ

It was Fin roused me, though he half-deafened me in the doing. I saw a rabbit once, brought in by a hound, that was paralyzed with fear. You would have thought its spine was broken, but no. Yet it lay in the hunter's hands, unmoving, while he wrung its neck. I was that rabbit, until Fin put his beak into my ear and shrieked. It flung me off the ground, and I realized that if I could jump so violently at a loud noise, then I was not paralyzed after all. Feeling returned to my limbs. The pain in my cheek flared. Thought returned.

"They'll have the whole of Emain Macha at the gate to witness my downfall," I muttered. I got to my feet, shaky still with shock, and made my way back to the road.

It didn't take me long to find what I sought. I had to crouch now to ease through the little door in the wall, but I did so in privacy, for no sentry was there to discover my plight. Once inside the embankment, I put my head down and ran, Fin's heavy flight leading the way.

Ξ

"Everybody out."

One hand over my cut cheek, I barged into my room and sent the two startled waiting women hurrying toward the door.

"Find Roisin," I called to their retreating backs. "Send her to me at once."

It was not long before she strode into the room, as bracing as a stiff wind off the sea. I have no doubt Roisin saved my life that day, simply by being who she is. Poor old Tullia would have wept over me as one already in the grave and begun a tender deathwatch. But Roisin was all angry defiance. In her presence, the warrior within me began to stir.

"Skies on fire, what happened to you!" she demanded, thinking only of my cut cheek. She pulled my hand away, gave the wound a quick once-over. "I know Cathbad is away, but there must be another druid here wise in healing. I'll find someone."

She was almost gone before my mind caught up with her.

"Wait, Roisin." Cathbad I would trust—not because I was entitled to his personal care as Conchobor's wife, but because of the kindness he had shown me from childhood. But the others...Abhartach's lies would have spread through Emain with the speed of all gossip. And the poets were, after all, akin to the druids, brothers on different branches of the same tree of knowledge.

"I don't want anyone to know I am here," I said.

Bless her heart, she didn't miss a beat.

"I'll get water and bandaging," she said briskly, then she paused once more in the doorway. "Luaine, was anyone here besides Ana and Grian when you came?"

"No."

"I think I'd best bring them back, don't you? Their mouths run faster than your fathers' horses."

I don't know what passed between Roisin and the other women, but when they returned with her, burdened with kettles of water and trays of food, they kept their lips pressed shut and their eyes averted. They put down their loads and with a single furtive glance at Roisin, scuttled away.

"I don't think we need worry about them now, my lady. I put the very fear of the Morrigu into them!"

She turned her attention to my face then, lighting several lamps and fussing with their placement while I tried to put words

to the enormity of the disaster that had befallen me. The cut was
the least of my worries. Roisin put a fingertip to my lips.
"First things first. Let me tend to this. Then you have a little
something to boost your strength, and you can tell me the whole
tale."

The shard was still embedded in my cheek. Roisin ripped one of
Conchobor's good linen sheets into strips, and gave me a pad to
press against my cheek and stem the bleeding as she removed it.

As it turned out, there was little bleeding to worry about.
"The cut is not deep," she pronounced, relief escaping in a sigh.
"The shard is quite small, after all." She looked at the object in her
hand. "Looks like a piece of crockery, or…" A frown creased her
forehead as she moved the shard into the lamplight. "There's something dark along the edge here. Not dried blood, I don't think."

A tendril of fear, the caress of a cold finger, brushed the pit of
my stomach.

"Wrap it up, Roisin, and keep it for now. And wash the cut well,
however shallow it is. Don't worry about hurting me."

To be truthful, the pain took me by surprise. How could a
shallow cut, not much worse than I had given myself more than
once with a kitchen knife, burn so ferociously? The first touch of
water reawakened the sensation of hot stingers drilling into my
flesh. I gritted my teeth and tried to keep silent, wanting to hide
my suffering from Roisin.

Suffering, I called it. I hadn't even scratched the surface of
pain.

Ξ

The angry flush that had appeared on Roisin's cheeks at the first
mention of the "boon" the brothers demanded of me spread as

I talked, so that by the end of my tale she was red as a turkey wattle.

"It all happened so fast," I concluded, my throat suddenly thick with tears. "I don't know what I did wrong." If I had only been more experienced, more clever, surely I would have found a way to turn aside their wrath.

"What *you* did wrong!" Roisin fair exploded. "The answer to that is easily told: Not one single thing!" The force of her indignation lifted her onto her feet where she stood, fists clenched, black eyes snapping. "It is those vicious, ill-begotten wolves who have done wrong, and not you!"

Slowly the truth of Roisin's words sank into my heart. I might be cursed, but I did not have to accept the blame for it.

"The real question," I said slowly, "is what to do now." I felt like a trapped badger, shut into my room with all of Emain waiting to watch the show.

The fire in her eyes faded to warm concern. "How do you feel now, Luaine? Are you well?"

I considered. My cheek hurt unceasingly, but it grumbled rather than screamed now that the dressing was done. I did not feel ill or even particularly weak. On the heels of that realization came an image that filled me with longing: a long crescent of beach, a rolling green plain, a house that looked out over both. And I knew Roisin was seeing the same place.

"Let's go home."

≡

We arrived near dusk under an overcast sky that promised rain after all. My cheek hurt fiercely—each thud of the horse's hooves bringing a jolt of fresh pain—but I wasn't thinking of that now.

I was looking at Dun Dealgan—at what was left of Dun Dealgan—and wondering if it was even habitable.

It had been torched. The whole south side was burned away, leaving a yawning hole and blackened timbers. Close to half the thatch had gone up. No doubt the house had been looted before they set the fire. Who had been caught there, I wondered, and fallen to Maeve's men?

We soon discovered that at least some remained, and that while the house had been abandoned, Dun Dealgan itself had not. We were in my room, in fact, relieved to find that the north of the house, though redolent with smoke, was undamaged, when a hesitant voice called out.

"Lady Luaine?" It was the stableboy, who had recognized my horse in the yard and come looking for me. His awed manner made it plain the king's message about our wedding had arrived. "I'll see to your horses and fetch someone for you," he blurted out and promptly disappeared.

Roisin was busy making up my bed. The place had indeed been looted but apparently in a hurry, for they had taken only the jewelry chests and small valuables and not bothered with linens or clothing. "Well, at least we will eat tonight," she said, shaking out the blankets with brisk precision. "But tomorrow, Luaine, we should go to my father's home. My family will welcome you, and small though it is, it is cheerier than this place."

I did not say it, but I couldn't see what need I had for cheer. I had, after all, come home to die. As if to remind me of that fact, my cheek flared once more, and I suddenly felt ill and shivery. It has started, I thought, and my hand flew to my face, searching for the first signs of the blemishes. It found none, but I discovered then that my skin radiated heat.

By the time Berach hurried in, I had crawled under the covers and was content to let Roisin speak with him. And from him we learned a thing that both grieved and moved me.

"Cuchulainn made it clear that we were to save the people, not the house," he apologized. "It angered me to let them in while we had any men standing, but fighting to the last would not have changed the outcome. As it is, we were able to get almost everyone out and safely into the countryside." All but two: Eirnin, who had died only the day before, worn out at last from illness and old age, and Tullia, who would not leave even at the point of a sword and had finally been carried bodily, cursing and struggling, from the grounds. "She snuck away that night and made her way back," marveled Berach. "The next day Maeve's army reached Dun Dealgan. We were putting up what resistance we could when I saw Tullia come flying out from the back kitchen, screaming like a madwoman, with a joint cleaver in each hand. And by my head she made a brave end, sinking one into the chest of a fellow who was like to twice her height before they cut her down."

Old Tullia. What had made her do such a thing, and her a slave?

I had not been sure how to explain our sudden arrival. Berach seemed to assume I had simply come to check on my holdings, but could not fathom that we had traveled alone. "Where is the Lady Luaine's retinue?" he asked Roisin. "Surely the Queen travels with an honor guard?" I made a sudden decision and sat up in the bed to reveal my hurt cheek. Berach's eyes widened, but he said nothing.

"The king is in Tara, Berach, and I have learned that I have enemies in Emain. I came here seeking protection, until…" Until Conchobor returns, I implied, but I did not imagine even the king could help me now. I blessed the stars that had put Berach in charge of Dun Dealgan. If there was loyalty to be had among my father's men, it would be here.

The arms master's face grew grim and cold. If he had questions, he kept them to himself.

"You will be safe here, my lady. I pledge my life on it." The task before him now clear, Berach strode from the room without another word.

I would not be safe. There was no place now that was safe for me. But I would at least be undisturbed.

☰

The night and then the day passed and still there were no blemishes. However, the cut on my cheek, far from improving, had become a swollen fiery torment, and the fever that gripped me was impossible to hide from Roisin. Nor could she hide her dismay from me.

"I don't understand," she said. The wet cloth she laid on my head eased the pounding in my temples, but even that light pressure, where it lay on the swelling by my left eye, heightened the throb in my cheek. "A cut this size should not cause such pain."

I had come to my own conclusion about that. "I think this must be the curse, Roisin. Not three blemishes—only this one."

She rose to her feet. "Curse or not, you need better tending than I can give you. There must be someone here wise in healing. I'll ask Berach."

It was Tullia who had treated my childhood scrapes and illnesses.

But Roisin was right; there must be others. I didn't give a wise woman's herbals any odds at all against a poet's curse, but Roisin felt she had to try, and it would do no harm.

In fact it helped, a little. At least the willow tea brought the fever down a bit and helped me sleep. But the old woman's poultice, which Roisin changed religiously three times that night, didn't touch the infection that had taken hold. By morning I could smell that it had gone bad, and the tears that welled up in Roisin's dark eyes as she held up the lamp to look only confirmed what I already knew.

"Take the lamp away; it hurts my eyes," I said. "There's nothing more to be done, or said." I closed my eyes, trying to ride out the pain that stabbed deep in my face when I spoke or moved my head. I drifted. I was beginning to be resigned to the thought of death, to see it, in fact, as a welcome relief from this waking nightmare. If death was inevitable, I thought, then let it come swiftly.

"I only wish the king could know the truth about me, Roisin. That my good name could be protected."

"Will he be back yet, Luaine?" she asked.

I tried to count the days. Fever and pain make it hard to think.

"No, I don't think so. But would he believe…" My eyes flew open.

"Fintan. Roisin, get Fintan. He saw everything. He will find Cathbad and tell him the true tale."

Ξ

I had tried to leave Fin at Emain Macha, knowing I would not be fit to care for him. But he would not stay, flapping his black wings all the way to Dun Dealgan beside us. Now he was off again, bearing my message, and I had only to endure until the end. I thought with envy now of my mother's quick death and guessed it would not be long before I sought out the kindness of the knife myself.

Chapter 17
Cathbad's Son

Someone was groaning, a terrible sound, the voice thin like a child's and jagged with despair. It frightened me, and I wished Roisin would see to whoever it was and quiet them.

"Luaine, wake up."

I started, saw a monstrous outline before me, and realized at the same time that it was myself making that fearful noise. I clamped my teeth down hard, and the voice died in my throat.

"Who is it?"

The lamps flared up, and I saw it was no monster but a tall man who stood before me—a man with a raven on his shoulder.

"Cathbad?"

"No." He eased his long legs down beside my low bed so I could see him better. A young man with fair hair pulled straight back rather than hanging down, a pleasant, bright face free of beard or mustache and eyes that seemed to look right into my soul. "I am Geanann, Cathbad's son. He is unable to come to you, but has sent me in his stead. I am not so powerful a druid as he, of course," and here he smiled, almost apologetically, "but my healing arts are stronger. I have come to see what might be done for you." He leaned over me, and with one smooth gesture eased me onto my side so that my cheek lay exposed to his sight. I tensed—I could not bear, now, the least touch upon it—but he did not try. For a long moment he just looked, not seeming to notice the smell of rot that must have assailed him.

When he sighed and sat back on his heels, I dared a question. "What could you possibly do? I have been cursed."

"Cursed?" The snort that escaped him would have been a laugh, if it had not been so full of anger and derision. "If those two knew anything about real curses, they would not bandy them about so freely. Put curses out of your mind." He rose to his feet and began to pace about the little room, suddenly agitated. "You have been poisoned. No ordinary wound could go septic and spread so quickly. If I knew what Abhartach used…"

I heard a hiss of indrawn breath, and Roisin stepped forward, fumbling in her pouch. She pulled out a wrapped piece of linen and thrust it at Geanann. "I pulled that from her cheek. Could there be poison still on it?"

Geanann unwrapped it gingerly, eyed the little shard of crockery under the lamplight, sniffed at it. He scratched at it with his blade. Then he wiped it on the linen, dripped a bit of water on it and examined the result closely. To my alarm, he once licked it—a quick touch of the tongue that I thought I must have imagined until I heard Roisin's involuntary gasp.

He stood then as if lost in thought, and as the minutes dragged on, the pain roared back into my face in a fierce wave and licked against the inside of my skull, and I fought to hold back that mewing groan that spoke to me of death.

≡

The choice he finally put to me was clear enough. He could, just possibly, save my life, but the pain of it would be greater than anything I would experience in the course of merely dying.

Or, if I chose not to endure such an ordeal, his draughts could ease my passing to the next world, which would take place in a matter of days.

"How much greater?" I asked, dreading his reply, but he shook his head.

"It is not given us to measure the degrees of pain as we can measure the shadow's length," he said. "I will have to cut away the dead flesh and then cauterize the edges. After that, you will have a long slow battle as the poison drains and the wound heals. And at the end, a wide scar that will disfigure the left side of your face."

The revulsion and fear I felt as I tried to picture the surgery was paralyzing. The skin of my cheek was now so stretched with swelling it felt near to splitting open, and so exquisitely tender that even the accidental brush of cloth against it made me cry out. Marshaling any other thought was almost more than I could manage—yet deep in my fevered brain an uneasy question was fighting its way to the surface.

I raised my hot eyes to his and saw that he was waiting.

"Why do you offer me a choice?" I demanded. "If life is indeed within my grasp, however difficult the pathway, why should I choose death?"

There was a silence while he studied me and seemed to search for words.

"My father said you would need the whole truth, ill though you be. He says you have a mind that seeks understanding."

Suddenly the real question was plain to me.

"Geanann, why has Conchobor not come? If he knows I kept faith with him, why does he not come to me?"

He told it as gently as he could, but there are some truths that cannot really be softened.

"When the king married you, Luaine, it was not your welfare he was thinking of, nor even your beauty, whatever he may have said."

I lay in my bed and closed my eyes against his kind face as he laid out what Cathbad had discovered. I understood now how it was possible to die of shame.

The king did not want me.

He had never wanted me, only my lands and the strength of my father's men and our herds and riches. And there was none of Cuchulainn's family left but myself to stand in the king's way. He had hired Abhartach and his brother to get rid of me, and was even now riding in a supposed rage to their house to kill them, thus ensuring they would never be tempted to let slip his secret.

"So you see," Geanann concluded, "if it is life that you choose, it is not clear what life awaits you. The king expects that you will succumb to the 'curse,' and there is no telling how it will be if, instead, you recover and return to Emain Macha."

"I will never return to him," I gritted. Tears welled up under my lids and scalded their way down to my pillow. I hadn't the strength left to feel anger at Conchobor's betrayal, but despair feeds on weakness and it washed over me now like the surf breaking over a rock. All I had to do was to let go, and let it take me…

"Luaine." Geanann's hand rested on mine, long fingers wrapping about my wrist, the pressure of them calling me back to him. Reluctantly, I opened my eyes and was grateful to see in his neither pity nor contempt, but only compassion.

"I cannot choose for you. But I will say that if it is life you decide to follow, Cathbad and I will help you to find a new path."

"Cathbad serves the king," I said bitterly.

"Cathbad serves Ulster," he corrected. "And Conchobor's kingship, whatever his personal faults, has been strong. Ulster cannot afford to lose him now, Luaine. Not with your father gone. But neither will Cathbad leave you unaided."

Ξ

I could not force my brain to work. The rack and chill of fever, the deep bite of my wound, the debilitating sense of shame—they pushed me toward the easy course. To let go and be at ease. But Geanann had offered me a different road, a harder road, and I owed it to him to at least consider it well.

"I need Fintan and some time alone," I said. I did not think Fin had anything new to show me, but I thought his white feather might help me find the thread of my thought.

And so it did. The white feather blazed out in the dim room against deepest black. And my thoughts did indeed find something to grip onto there, a focus that gave me some distance from the pain. I fixed my eyes on Fintan's white feather, and there swelled out of its small bright beacon a wheeling dance of memories.

They were random, at first, fleeting scraps of my childhood. My father's apple feat. My mother singing. Sunrise over the sea, the Cooley Hills still blue with night's shadow. The time my father sneezed with a mouthful of ale and it shot out his nose, and I could not finish my meal for laughing. The little white asters that nestle into the grass around our house like fallen stars.

But the memories all ended in death. I saw my brother, the eager young flame of his life stamped out in the service of another's vengefulness. My mother, throwing herself into the grave without a thought for what was left behind. And then it was Deirdriu swimming out of Fin's white light. Her sorrowful violet eyes glowed like jewels before me, charging me with some burden or message. And then they vanished in a rising tide of blood, and I remembered how when she lay there, her head shattered and her soul finally free, Conchobor was not grieved but only angered. Cheated of his prize.

And then at last the anger blazed within me, for Deirdriu and for myself too. Was I worth so little, then, that my life should be tossed aside for a man whose greed had swelled beyond bounds? My father had not been king of a great province, but he had shone brighter than Conchobor ever could, nor was he one to betray the memory of a friend.

"Call them in, Fin. Geanann and Roisin both."

And when they had entered, and Geanann had knelt by my bed to hear me speak, I forced my words to rise above the pain they caused me and sound clear in the little room.

"Cuchulainn's line will not die out from Conchobor's treachery. I swear by the gods we honor, I will defy him, king though he be. I will live."

CHAPTER 18
FRIENDS AND HELPERS

Two years it has been since Geanann gave me a draught that made me dreamy and limp, carried me out into the bright light of the noonday sun, wound straps across my arms and legs and set Berach to hold my head while two other stout men pinned down the rest of me. Two years and still my mind skitters away from the memory in blind refusal. There are some things that cannot be relived, nor recounted.

Nor can they be forgotten, however we may wish to. Not without Cathbad's draught of oblivion. Geanann offered it to me, you know—but I turned him down. I didn't know what other memories might be lost along with the pain, and as you must realize by now, I am not one to turn my back on knowledge. Here is a memory I do not mind sharing: when at last Geanann was done and he laid his fiery blade aside, Berach loosed his hold on me with a groan that was clogged thick with tears. And I hovered on the edge of a blackness that might well have been death and yearned for it to blot out the world, for the agony was a live beast in me still and I shook with a violence that made my teeth clatter. But Geanann poured cool water from a pitcher onto clean linen, and bathed my eyes and spoke in a quiet murmur, and when nausea overcame me his strong arms held me firm as the sickness spattered on the ground, and he washed my mouth afterward as tenderly as a mother. And then he scooped me up and carried me back to bed. The blackness did close over me then, and I slept the sleep of utter exhaustion.

Sleep was my friend and waking a torment in the measureless time that followed. But never did my eyes open without seeing Roisin or Geanann at my side, ready with the draught that quieted my body and lulled me back to the darkness. Such strange sleep. I swooped and sank in my bed, and behind my eyelids colors and images bloomed and faded like the dancing lights that sometimes paint the northern sky.

It was the poppy did that. Geanann told me later he had got it from a healer he met while studying in Alba, a man who had learned its uses in a faraway land where the sun blazed so hot you could burn the soles of your feet just walking on the earth. His small store was precious, though, and he soon switched me to a weaker brew of local herbs. And so I found myself truly awake and able to really look at the man who had hurt me so terribly. Bright-faced Geanann. That's what they call him, and one look was enough to show the reason. His mother must have been very fair, for he had little of Cathbad's darkness about him, but was golden-haired with a boyish high color to his cheeks. Only his eyes spoke of his father, for they were a deep storm-gray where one expected blue.

I made to shift my position—I had lain so long in one place that the straw was packed hard against the bed boards and my back was complaining—and instantly it was my whole body complaining, and loudly. No doubt it showed on my face.

"Sore?" asked Geanann.

"Yes," I said. Tried to say. It came out a hoarse rasp and felt about the same. I ached everywhere, as if I had been through a battle. I suppose I had.

"For a woman drugged and sick, you fought like a bear," he said apologetically. Then, perhaps regretting the memories he had sparked, he turned back to the present.

"You are doing marvelously well, despite your aches. The fever is nearly gone, and the swelling on your cheek is improving already." He hoisted up my shoulders and gave me a spoonful of thick syrup, warm and sweet with honey. "For your throat," he said.

I took stock of myself and realized what he said was true. My face hurt unrelentingly, but the skin no longer felt stretched tight as a drumskin. My head felt clearer and my limbs lay still, free from the quaking grip of fever. I would live.

Geanann had saved me. I cleared my throat experimentally and looked up at him, meaning to say my thanks. Instead I surprised myself. "You don't look like a druid."

That made him laugh, and the merry sound of it lifted my spirits in a way nothing else could have. It was long since there had been any laughter in my life, and I felt my own lips curl into a careful smile.

"Doubtless that's because I am not yet fully vested, but have attained only the first order," he replied. "In ten years' time, I promise you, I shall look as severe and wise as Cathbad himself."

Three times seven years of study it takes to become a master with the wisdom to guide kings and train apprentices. Geanann had the eyes already: observant, perceptive, quietly commanding. But even with his hairline shaved back in the tonsure of the master druid, I doubted he would ever resemble Cathbad.

A slow tickly motion on my cheek distracted me, and I made—wincing—to lift a hand and brush the stray hair away. Geanann stopped me, leaning over my face with a thin straw in his hand. "Back to work, you," I heard him mutter, and there was a momentary twinge as the straw poked at my wound.

"You'd like to know who it is I am addressing," he stated as he sat back on his heels. "That was one of my helpers."

"What helpers?" Could he speak with the spirits, I wondered, glancing uneasily into the rafters.

"Maggots," he said cheerily.

Maggots. Every flyblown carcass and writhing mass of bad meat I had ever seen appeared in my mind's eye, and my own face alongside them. My stomach did a slow roll.

"Roisin thought the same as you. I almost had to fight her to get at you with them."

"You *put* them in me?" My voice was back, loud and clear and full of indignant revulsion. "You put *maggots* in me?!"

"Be glad I did," he answered calmly, serious now. "They are cleaning out the poison and dead flesh in the deep places I could not reach, and they have very likely saved the sight in your left eye."

"But—"

"But what? Are they hurting you? Would you prefer the clumsy slicing of my knife?"

No. Not that.

I took a deep breath and put my mind to the facts. My cheek felt better, not worse. I could not even tell the maggots were there. Perhaps most importantly, I had come to trust in Geanann's skill.

"But what happens when they run out of dead flesh?" I imagined them burrowing into my living tissue. It made me shudder.

"They cannot eat healthy flesh," he assured me. "When they are done, they will come out."

Something to look forward to.

Ξ

For two more days I rested and gained strength, and soon I was well enough to notice that Geanann and Roisin grew more uneasy by the hour. By the time they came to speak to me, I had figured out the reason.

"Conchobor will be sending men here, won't he?"

Geanann nodded. "And soon. It is coming on ten days since you left Emain Macha. Not to mince words, he will think he has left you ample time to die."

"And if they find me alive?"

I watched his mouth flatten into a grim line and knew that his thinking matched my own. "Having begun this charade, I do not think Conchobor can afford to leave you alive and risk having his treachery revealed. The warriors remember how he misused Fergus to his own ends to regain Deirdriu. He will lose their trust entirely if this comes out."

I understood then—and the bitterness of it was sour in my mouth—that only the king's treatment of his men was at issue here. It was for the betrayal of Cuingedach and Abhartach, and for my father's memory, they would not forgive him. There would be no hot uprising on my account.

Ξ

It does not come easy to a warrior's child to flee in the face of an enemy. My father's spirit cried out for me to stand, and at the thought a fierce defiant joy sang in me. To die defending my home, to make a brave end—it was bright and clean and strong, compared to a murky future that seemed to have shrunk into skulking dishonor.

But it was not just my own life I held in my hand. Berach and his men might defend Dun Dealgan against the first troops to arrive from Emain Macha, but they would not withstand the might of Ulster for long. And I was no warrior, despite my hot blood. I would not spend others' lives for a hopeless cause.

It was Berach's idea to knock down the flimsy inner walls and destroy more thatch to make the house as uninhabitable as possible. "They'll find the place abandoned, looted and wide open to the weather," he proposed. "So it's not likely they'll install a new chieftain without a long rebuilding. That will buy you some time, at least."

Ξ

Roisin had ridden ahead to let her family know we were coming, and as Geanann and I prepared to follow I tried once more.

"Geanann, honestly, there's no need for the cart. Orlagh has a nice smooth pace and—"

"You are not ready to ride," he cut me off.

He was right—my legs were trembly already, just from being out of bed—but I bristled at his tone. The friendly warmth had gone, replaced by a voice designed to shut down discussion. Druid authority speaks. And I might have been cowed by it, was I not still so full of bottled-up battle lust. I let it out now.

"I will *not* leave this place in a god-cursed cart! Bad enough that I am running from my own home. It is the daughter of Emer the Fair and Cuchulainn of Muirthemne who speaks now, and I tell you I will ride from here with my head held high or I will stay in my bed and wait for them to kill me!"

I untied Orlagh's lead line from the back of the cart and flung myself into the saddle. My cheek flared at the sudden exertion, but I paid it no mind. I was missing something. "Where is my sword?"

"Here, my lady."

It was Berach. He astonished me by presenting the sword formally, laid across his two great fists, and then stepping back to drop to one knee, hand over his heart. "At your service, always," he said.

I could feel the tears pressing behind my eyes. But I made them stay there. It is no way to receive a warrior's oath, with weeping. I drew myself straight in the saddle and laid my own hand over my breast. "There is no man I trust more, Berach," I said. I gazed down at his pale fierce eyes, his blunt face, and knew the words to be true.

I buckled on the sword, nodded to Berach and wheeled Orlagh about. Then I looked over my shoulder to Geanann.

"Are you ready, then?"

"At your service," he murmured. He had an odd look on his face, and I could not tell whether his words were ironic or not.

Berach grinned and raised a hand in salute as I kicked my mare into a canter.

I did not look back again.

Ξ

I did regret my haughty words, though. To speak thus to one of the Wise Ones, a man to whom I owed my life! He had no need to be spending his days looking after a beleaguered girl, I reminded myself.

And so I soon reined in my horse and waited for Geanann to come alongside me. He said nothing, merely gazed at me with that neutral, unreadable expression that is part of a druid's training.

"Cathbad warned me once against misplaced pride," I said. "My words did not match the respect I hold for you, and I am ashamed to have spoken them. I beg your forgiveness." My voice trembled a little at the end, and the tears did prick out in my eyes now, but I kept them trained on Geanann.

I swear it is like watching the sun sail out from behind the clouds when he smiles. The whole world is suddenly brighter.

"Conchobor should have made you a true queen," he said. "You would have been formidable."

It was the last thing I expected to hear. I ducked my head, flustered and at a complete loss for words.

"Shall we slow down to a walk now?" Geanann continued. "It is entirely your decision, of course, but for myself I have seen enough blood pouring from that wound, which is barely knit together, and would prefer that it not be jarred open."

It was a slow trip to Brocc's homestead. I followed Geanann's pace without complaint, and the sun slanted low in the sky when we finally clip-clopped into the smith's yard. To my dismay, the half-day ride had worn me right down to a nub—but I was at least unbloodied.

CHAPTER 19
THE HIDDEN ROAD

A skilled smith is an honored craftsman, and Brocc's home was prosperous and comfortable. Roisin's sisters and aunt plied me with hot food, warm baths and a stream of bright magpie chatter that seemed to flow from their mouths as naturally as breath.

Two days in that busy, cheerful home had done much to restore my strength, but nothing to quiet my mind.

I saw now what a strange and isolated upbringing I'd had. Roisin could scarcely comprehend how alone I was in the world. Though her own mother had died in her last childbirth, Roisin had grown up within a great web of family. Her father's widowed sister and her son had lived with them since Roisin was a nursling; her mother's two sisters had each taken a turn at fostering her. There were uncles to share in the working of the lands and the training of unruly boys, young cousins who played and fought and slept together like puppies. It was enough to make me weep.

But the faults of my childhood were beside the point. I had to decide what to do next, and soon. Yet all the paths before me, it seemed, led to a dead end.

Geanann's patient ear had helped trace the paths, but he had not found me a better one. My choices boiled down to two.

If I moved quickly, I could try to hold Dun Dealgan. It was mine, after all. We would not last long against attack by the combined forces of Ulster, but perhaps Conchobor would not risk an outright assault. He might not want to test his chieftains' loyalty by setting them against the orphaned child of their greatest champion. Still, what then? Would I reveal his plot? Alone, I had no proof, only wild accusations. Cathbad would not support my claim—he had made it clear he was not willing to overturn the throne of Ulster and risk a further weakening of leadership at this vulnerable time. Without these accusations, I had no grounds for divorce. So I would remain Conchobor's estranged wife, and my life would remain the sole impediment to his securing of Muirthemne.

"He wants that title free and clear for his grown sons," Geanann had agreed solemnly. "In the natural course of things, you would outlive him and retain your lands. He will not let that happen."

So, that was one possible future: locked behind the gates of my own home, watching always for the assassin's blade, the poisoned drink, the sudden attack, with no real chance of prevailing.

Or I could seek refuge with my uncles in Leinster. My mother's brothers had been spared by Cuchulainn and they knew it. They had never fought directly against my father. We had not met, but I was their blood relation—surely they would give me sanctuary?

"They will want you to join your lands to their family," said Geanann. "Will you war against Ulster on their behalf to secure Muirthemne?"

Why not? I thought hotly. It is Ulster has turned its hand against me. There was warrior enough in me to lust after revenge.

Except when I tried to picture the outcome, either victory or defeat, an image rose up in its stead. It was the row of heads Conall Cearnach had laid out at my mother's feet I saw, taken in vengeance for my father's death. Buzzing with flies, rank with gore, they filled me with weary disgust. Death for death for death. I had had enough of it.

Would I go, then, to my uncles, without lands or herds? I would not be destitute—there was the buried cache my mother had shown me, a bride's portion and more, she had said. I could pay for my keep. Live on the edges of the family, a single woman bound to gratitude. Or I could marry. It is not legal, of course, for a woman to have more than one husband—but that would not preclude an informal bond until Conchobor's death freed me. But what man would want me? My face was ruined—the shocked expressions of Roisin's family when they first clapped eyes on me had made that clear. Geanann said that in time the scar would tighten together and the angry color fade, but he admitted it would always be a broad dusky track across my face. So: no beauty, no lands and the enmity of the King of Ulster. I was not likely to be beating off the suitors.

Was this what I had struggled back from the edge of death for? It was a chance, I reminded myself. Every peasant in Ireland faced worse prospects and a harder life. But I was no peasant, and the role of refugee repelled me.

Ξ

How long had it been since I had rambled the countryside with Fintan? My lovely plain swelled and dipped before me, its long vista dotted here and there with farmholdings but the peace of it unbroken. The clang of Brocc's hammer and the bustle of his household fell away behind me, and for a moment I let myself imagine I was a carefree girl again, a girl confident of her place in the world. A girl with no more pressing task than to slip the lead of her tutors and taskmasters and give herself to sweet daydreams.

I was no longer that girl.

But the anxious useless circling of my own thoughts was driving me mad. I needed to escape them for a while. I needed to be quiet, inside and out. And so I walked, and my legs, weak at first from disuse, soon found their easy stride and strength. I watched the clouds scud across the sky, felt the wind lift my hair, startled and then laughed as a grouse exploded out of a thicket in noisy alarm. Fintan flew before me, lighting down to investigate where he would, but never far away.

Geanann's astonishing words echoed in my head: "Conchobor seeks your death because he fears you. His first intent may have been to keep you as a powerless bride, but he soon saw you would not submit to his domination for long."

"I gave him no cause," I protested. "I was obedient to his will."

Geanann smiled. "It is nothing that you did," he said. "You have the mark of power on you. My father saw it when you were but a child."

Cathbad, apparently, believed I had a worthy future. But all my straining and grasping had failed to reveal it.

So I walked, and let my mind slowly empty, as I had done nearly every day as a child at Dun Dealgan. I let my thoughts reel away into the clouds, leaving the inner turmoil behind, stretching out instead to the vista surrounding me. I walked, and the rhythm of my legs and heart and breath seemed to match some great heartbeat of the earth. Thrumming through grass and rock and tree, through every finch and beetle, I felt the vital energy of a world that does not question its existence but seeks only to live. It hummed in me as well. I was alive and well and part of this green and golden plain. For the moment, it was enough.

When my legs tired and my cheek's complaints from the jarring of my own tread became insistent, I lay in the turf and closed my eyes. The autumn grass was tall and plumed, no longer bright with summer flowers, but dotted still with flat white yarrow blossoms and the pink stalks of redshank. I breathed in the earth smell, rich and damp, the clean freshness of grass. I allowed myself to be happy.

The answer, when it came, was so obvious that there was no thunderclap of inspiration but only quiet certainty. One moment it was unthought of, the next inevitable, as if all my life had led me to this one place. The longer I held it in my heart, the more right it felt.

I knew now what I wanted for my life. It sang to me with every step as I made my way back to Brocc's house. It remained only to see if Cathbad would grant it. I thought he would. He had, after all, given me his raven. A druid's raven.

Ξ

Geanann did not even wait for me to speak. He took one look at me, and his face lit up in that sunny grin.

"You have found your road, I see."

I smiled back. I had best get used to such second-guessing.

"And you already know what it is, I suppose."

"That I do. My father foresaw this end for you long ago, if not the manner of your arriving there. But it was not permitted that I should suggest it to you."

I thought I understood. The druid's life is not to be chosen as a refuge from difficulties but rather from heartfelt desire—a calling, if you like. Still, it gave me an uneasy feeling, to think of Cathbad knowing my future all this time. *Foretelling.* I'd had a taste of it myself, and I did not think I was much enamored of this particular druid gift.

Evidently Geanann felt differently. "Cathbad believes you have the potential to be a seer. He says even as a child you showed signs of the gift."

Something sounded wrong in his voice. I glanced up quickly, searching his face for the hidden meaning, and was met with sheepish acknowledgment.

"Your perception is true. I cannot quite keep the envy from my voice, though I swear it is without any trace of malice. It is what I myself aspired to—to be one of the farseeing. Alas, it is not my gift."

"Your gift saved my life, Geanann," I said. "Do not expect me to value foresight over the skill and knowledge you have."

He nodded acknowledgment. "I have learned, for the most part, to be content with what I have been given. But you, Luaine—are you not pleased to have such a chance? Many consider the *fili* to be the highest branch of wisdom."

Who was I to argue with the sages? I kept silent for a bit, unsure of how to answer and even of my own feelings. But at last, as it nearly always does, my mind insisted on speaking its thoughts.

"What good has it ever done, Geanann?"

He looked startled. "What?"

"Prophecy. Foresight. What is the use of it? I cannot see that it ever saved anyone. My grandfather Forgall was a druid, and in his efforts to escape the prophecy that he would come to harm from my father, he put himself directly in harm's way. Does it not always end so, even in the old stories? And Deirdriu—Cathbad foresaw the bloodshed that would come to Ulster through her. Conchobor thought to avoid it by claiming her for himself, and look what followed!"

I paused, remembering. Painful memories, they were, and my voice wasn't more than a whisper as I told him.

"When I knew that my father was after killing his own son, what use was that to me or to him? I could not stop him from loosing the Gae Bolga, nor turn aside the spear."

CHAPTER 20
TREASURES FOUND

"There really is such a place?"

It seemed too good to be true, what Geanann described to me. Cluain-na-mBan: an island in a saltwater lagoon, floating on the mysterious edge between worlds, where the borders between land and water, ocean and lake, blended one into the other. It was a place held sacred to the sun god Mug Ruith. And here is the part that was a wonder to me—a community of druid women lived there. Only women: studying, teaching and talking to their gods.

"The Isle of Women is not a secret," smiled Geanann. "But its existence is kept quiet. Apparently you are not the first applicant for whom the island has been a refuge as well as a school. The family of an aspiring druid is not always well-pleased with her calling."

A druid was a person of high honor, whose status brought prestige to his or her family. Still, I could imagine that might be cold comfort to a husband whose home was neglected or to aging parents who counted on their daughter's labor.

On the Isle of Women I would be able to devote myself entirely to learning, far from the eyes and ears of Conchobor and his men.

Ξ

Somehow I had expected that, having found my path, it would now open before me as broad and smooth as a river. In truth, there were a hundred details and complications to sort out before I could begin the journey that would take me so far from my childhood home.

First among these was the problem of my wealth. I needed some of it to pay my way, and I was not about to leave any of it under the nose of Dun Dealgan's new master. Yet I could hardly travel for days on end with a cart full of treasure in tow—not if I wanted to arrive with anything to my name at all. No doubt Geanann's druid authority would protect us to some extent; still I was unwilling to trust my entire livelihood to the piety of robbers.

It was Roisin's father who came to my aid.

"Hide the bulk of it here," he urged. "We are far enough inland from the fort that you can come and go unnoticed. My sons and I will see to its safety."

I looked at him: black-haired, big-shouldered, and his two sons as brawny as himself. There is treachery in the world, as I well knew, but there is also honesty. This was a time for trust.

And so we prepared to raid my own treasure: myself, Geanann and Brocc's son Tomman—as silent a man as Roisin was talkative—to drive the ox-cart.

"But if we are noticed and questioned?" I fretted. Even circling widely around, eventually we would be in view of Dun Dealgan. I could not find the spot otherwise, nor get the cart up the hillside's overgrown slopes.

Geanann looked at me strangely.

"Do you suppose there are many in Ulster who would question the business of any druid, let alone Cathbad's son?"

When death breathes over you, you see people differently. I had met Geanann at a time when rank and authority meant little to me. I saw him now in Tomman's eyes: a man of power and knowledge. A man who spoke before kings and knew the will of the gods. He was a man to fear and respect, and I, who had put my very life in his hands once already, had allowed his kind manner to obscure that fact. I felt my cheeks color.

"In any case, we will not put my authority to such a test," he continued briskly, saving me a flustered apology. "Healing is not my only skill." And he walked out Brocc's gate and headed east.

I watched, completely baffled, until he disappeared from view. "What on earth is he up to? I thought we were ready to leave."

"Magic, my lady," a voice growled beside me. I turned to see Tomman at my elbow. He gave me the white-eyed look of a frightened horse. "He is making magic."

Ξ

And so he was. As we drew near to Dun Dealgan, the skies darkened over the ocean and, like a hand laid over a child's eyes, a thick fog crept inland to settle over my old home. We picked our way up the shoulder of the mountain in perfect sunshine, but when I looked back toward the coast I saw straight gray threads of rain driving down from the clouds into a pearly blanket that shrouded the land. My spine prickled and I looked at Geanann, riding ahead of me, with something close to alarm.

What did you think a druid was? I chided myself. It was the knowledge—the histories and lore and law—that called to me, not the magic and rites and sacrifices. Yet magic was a kind of knowledge too and a part of every druid's training. Would I one day find within myself the power to call up weather?

"My lady?" Tomman, resolutely averting his eyes from both the mists below us and the man who had made them, was looking to me for direction. We were well up the slope now, and it was time to put musings aside and look to the landmarks.

There was more in the caches than I had dared to hope. Four good-sized bundles there were: enough to fill the cart, enough to give me, landless and herdless as I was, the means to live for many years to come.

Though I was not quite herdless after all.

We had just started back along the narrow track that threaded down the hillside, when a commotion in the underbrush sent my hand flying to my sword. With a stifled curse, Geanann yanked a spear from the cart and pushed me behind him. We all three turned toward the sound, straining to identify the crashing that grew louder with every breath. Surely not men, I thought, and relaxed a little. Only a half-wit would attempt an ambush through a thorny wall of head-high gorse. Then we heard a bawl of frustration, and I knew.

Sure enough, minutes later a shaggy head thrust its way from the shrubbery. The cow shoved her way through, flattening the branches obstructing her path, and emerged beside us. A calf followed in her wake and nestled close to its mam's flank. Big brown eyes blinked at us, and we laughed. Half-wit indeed, I thought.

"She must have calved late and got separated from the herd," said Tomman. He turned to go, grabbing hold of the ox's harness and urging it forward against the weight of the laden cart, but I called to him to wait. Rummaging in the loaded cart, I pulled out one of the lengths of rope we had brought.

"These are my cattle, are they not?" I said. "I cannot go after my entire stock, but I see no reason not to bring along these two." And so we returned two more than we had started, and my new cow and her calf seemed content enough to leave the rough hills behind and follow us.

I gave the cow to Brocc's family, in thanks for their assistance. It was a handsome gift, for she was in full milk still. The calf I took with me. It was of an age to be weaned and would be a fine contribution to my new home.

Ξ

I was surprised to find Berach in Brocc's yard when we returned. Not with bad news, though; he and Brocc were sharing a jar of ale, both looking well content with the day.

"Lady Luaine," Berach said to me as I settled myself beside them. "I understand you have a long journey ahead. Would you allow me to accompany you, as your bodyguard?"

My first response was grateful relief. I had been nervous about traveling with Geanann alone—needlessly, perhaps, since he had traveled all over Ireland and over the sea as well, but still... Berach and Geanann together, though, would be a match for all but the largest band of robbers. But it was time I thought of others besides myself.

"You should not be away when Dun Dealgan changes hands," I pointed out. "You must be ready to report to your new chieftain and receive your duties. Surely a high position awaits you."

Berach's blunt face became cold as an ax-head. "I'll not be serving under any new lord of Dun Dealgan, nor under Conchobor himself. Will I kneel to a man I cannot respect?"

My heart sank. "But Berach," I protested, "will you go to Connaught, or serve some other king who fought against my father and your people?" I was so upset to think that Berach's loyalty to me had led him here, to lose his place and his home, that I did not at first notice his broad grin.

"Nay, my lady, do not fear." His red hand was raised placatingly and the stony anger had vanished from his face. "I will go to the new high king at Tara, if he will take me."

I blinked. There had not been a high king of Ireland in all my lifetime.

Geanann saw my bewilderment and stepped in. "It happened while you were sick, Luaine." Only Geanann could speak of what had befallen me in such a matter-of-fact way, as though I had suffered a simple bout of the red fever or a bad chest. "The druids held the bull-feast while Conchobor was at Tara, so that he and Ailill and Maeve would be witness to the high king's naming. They dreamed true. Berach just got the news at Dun Dealgan."

"Who is it then?" I asked.

Berach beat him to it. "It's young Lugaid of the Red Stripes, who was a pupil of your father's." The choice obviously pleased him. "I worked with the lad myself, betimes. You could see the quality in him, even then."

I remembered him—had been rather meanly jealous of him, in fact, for the three years he had shadowed my father. Back then Lugaid had sported a tousled shock of brown hair, a stringy youth's frame and the proud patchy beginning of a warrior's mustache. But Berach was right; he had a way about him—a blend of easy courtesy and confidence rare at that age. He had won me over. By ten I was daydreaming about our future marriage. Just childish storytelling, it was—yet if my life had followed a different track, it might have turned out so. And now Lugaid was king over all the provinces, and him barely twenty. I wondered if he felt capable of carrying the weight that had been put on his shoulders, or was he like I had been at Emain Macha—acting the part and hoping it would fool the powerful rulers who were now expected to bow to his young will.

I turned back to Berach. "He will need good men at his side, Berach, is what I am thinking. And if he has half the quality you say, he will see that your own worth is of the best and reward it well." He colored a bit and gave a curt nod of thanks.

"And I thank you for your kindness," I added. "We will welcome your company and your protection on our journey." I was speaking for Geanann without knowing his mind, but I was not about to consult him over this. I wanted Berach at my side.

"And that of myself as well." Roisin had appeared and spoke up briskly from over Berach's shoulder. I sighed. This was a conversation I had put off too long, but I had intended it to be private.

"Roisin, you can't come," I said. It spoke to the fierceness of her loyalty that I felt apologetic about doing what was, beyond doubt, the best for her. "Geanann has told me that at the island they prefer initiates to come alone. And besides, how will you ever start a family of your own if you are stuck on an island full of women? It's hardly a place to be finding a husband."

She smirked at me, black eyes full of mischief, and I found myself annoyed. Discomfited, rather—I had felt out of my depth in this entire conversation, and the sensation was not pleasant.

"I'll not be leaving you in that place until I'm sure it's all right," declared Roisin. "And as for the other, you can rest easy on my account. I have found myself a husband already. He's just after speaking to my father, and we'll be traveling on to Tara together once we see you safe to your new home."

Oh, I must have been a comical sight as I watched Roisin sidle up beside Berach and lace her arm through his. Like a gaping fool,

I must have looked, as my mind scrambled to catch up with her. It was Berach's face that told me I had, indeed, understood Roisin's words. He put his big paw over her hand and gazed down at her, and his ugly face was so transformed with tenderness and pride that you would hardly have recognized it.

"We saw a good deal of each other while you were at Dun Dealgan, Lady Luaine," explained Berach.

"And we liked what we saw!" finished Roisin, her eyes dancing.

Didn't I say she had good sense, my Roisin? At Emain Macha her eyes had been always on the most handsome of the young warriors. She would not have spared a glance for an older man like Berach, nor one so homely. But she recognizes treasure when it lands in her lap.

I stepped forward and wrapped an arm around each one. "You could not have chosen better, either of you." I stepped back and grinned at them both, and then we were all laughing, and I understood now how Geanann had at once envied and been glad for me. I could see how it would be for them: Roisin coming to rely on Berach's steady strength, himself lifted by her high spirits, the house gradually filling up with babies. "I am happy beyond words for you," I said, and I was. And didn't I have an exciting future of my own beckoning, one I had not dreamed possible? Still the old dreams die hard, and my new path looked a lonely one in that moment.

CHAPTER 21
THE ISLE OF WOMEN

What can I tell you of our long journey south? I had never traveled so far, nor even slept out of doors except at Beltane. Our road skirted the sea for the most part, but in the places where the slopes of the mountains pushed right down to the coast we traveled in thick forest. It was not the light woodland I was used to but a land of crowded, towering trees that shut out the light and obscured the surrounding country so that we could not tell what lay twenty paces ahead.

Geanann insisted we not travel too fast or too far in a day. It filled me with impatience each morning, but in the evenings I was glad of his caution, for as the hours stretched on, the scar in my cheek came alive. The second night was the worst; we were well into Leinster by then, very near to my uncles' lands in fact. My cheek pained me as it hadn't for many days, a hot insistent throb that made me despair of sleep.

He noticed, of course. I thought I had hidden my discomfort, but as I tossed in my blanket Geanann arrived at my side with a mug of some vile-smelling brew.

"The weather is changing," he said as he pressed the cup into my hand. "You may find your wound ever warns you of oncoming rain."

"I would rather be surprised," I muttered, but I took the draught, and I slept.

That was the last of the glorious weather we enjoyed that autumn. We woke to a gray drizzle that settled over the land like an unwelcome guest. In the days to come we had every kind of rain in existence, from a fine invisible mist that beaded on our hair and cloaks to lashing downpours that drenched us to the bone. One morning we picked our way through the forest in a silent silvery fog that billowed up from the wet ground like the very breath of the Otherworld, smelling of the secret rivers that run deep under the bones of the earth. A couple of times we were able to shelter for the night on a farmstead and dry out our things, but we skirted wide of any large duns. Berach was not the high king's man yet, and for myself I wished to avoid awkward questions.

Strangely, the weather was not able to dampen my spirits. My eagerness grew with every mile we traveled. I could hardly sleep on the last night of our journey, though we were warm around a farmer's hearth. It was a new life I would be greeting on the morrow, and my mind jumped like a flea between excitement and nerves.

Ξ

The storm swept over us before we had traveled an hour. It upset me as the other weather had not; I wanted to arrive dry and composed, not bedraggled and dripping. We were at the southeast tip of Ireland now; the mountains had been left behind for a flat open land dotted with cleared fields and farmsteads, and while our road was now broad and easy, there was nothing to shelter us from the driving wind that ripped across the plain. The calf bawled with fear at every crack of lightning, and we had to clutch our cloaks tight, for the storm seemed bent on tearing the clothes from our skin. I kicked Orlagh up beside Geanann and yelled into his ear.

"Are the gods angry with me, Geanann? Do they set their will against me?"

He smiled. Rain was streaming down his face, despite the heavy wool hood. "More like it is your new mistress," he shouted.

I stared at him in confusion. Was he saying she did not want me? How could he smile at such a thing?

"It takes determination to become a druid," he explained. "The Isle of Women is not easily approached. Not by those seeking initiation."

It was a test, then. She must be powerful, I thought, to call up a storm like this. Still, it seemed a silly effort. I tugged at Geanann's cloak.

"She could not suppose that weather would turn me back?"

His hoot of laughter was snatched away by the wind. "It turns back the weak of will and the frivolous of mind. If she knew you as I do, no doubt she would not have bothered!"

Ξ

There is a self-confidence that comes with a high name. I had grown up in the reflected light of the respect given to my parents. Without even thinking of it, I had known that my place in the world was assured. Now I was to stand, homeless and in hiding, before a high druidess, with nothing but my own self to recommend my worth. It made me feel naked.

She was waiting for us at the end of the causeway that joined the isle to the mainland. The storm had passed, and in the uncanny quiet that followed I could hear the steady dripping as branches and leaves shook off their burden of rainwater. The lake—only a small channel on this side—was a still gray mirror.

Tlachta was, well, not what I expected. In those days, my imagination patterned all druids after Cathbad. For one thing, Tlachta was shorter than me by a head, and I am not much above average height for a woman. And though her hair was gray and her forehead disconcertingly high from the shaved tonsure that marked her as a Master, she was by no means ancient. She was vigorous and womanly still, lush in the hip and breast, and when she turned to lead us onto the isle she walked with a grace that I thought might still turn a man's head.

Geanann greeted her as "daughter of the Sun" and that sent a thrill of apprehension through me. People used to whisper that my father was the son of the god Lugh, and as a girl I loved imagining it was true without ever believing it or letting it worry me one whit. But this was different; Tlachta was a stranger to me and a woman of power, and Mug Ruith a southern god I had barely heard of. In my mind, the great unknown that was my life here became even more unpredictable.

I could have spared myself that worry. It was not long before I learned that "daughter of the Sun" or "daughter of Mug Ruith" is a title of office, given to every mistress of Cluain-na-mBan. While Tlachta is a woman to inspire awe, she is not truly born of the sun god, but rather dedicated to his service.

We walked into a dense wall of trees, an apparent forest which soon thinned out to reveal a sizeable community: lime-washed houses, both round and rectangular, a stable and beyond them, cultivated fields and pastures. It all looked so…*normal.*

Tlachta was brisk and assured in her hospitality, and there was soon a bustle about us. To my surprise a man came to see to our horses and the calf, and then we were shown to our respective

quarters: the apprentices' house for me, the men's guesthouse for
Geanann and Berach and a women's guesthouse for Roisin. I could
see she was irked to be sent there, but whether she wished to sleep
beside Berach or me, I could not tell. Berach, most likely.

The apprentices' house was a long low building, filled with two
rows of simple wattle bed frames and little else.

"This one is free and away from the door," said the girl who led
me there. "You'll be out of the draft."

I would be sharing my sleeping space, by the looks of it, with
nearly twenty other girls and women. Coming as I did from a
small wealthy family, I found it unpleasantly crowded. But the
straw was fresh, so I nodded my thanks to the fellow who carried
in my trunk and set it at the foot of the bed. Another man! I had
jumped to a foolish conclusion, I realized; it is the druids who are
women here, not every soul who works for them.

"If you have more things, there is a storage room attached to
the back of the house," the girl said. I thought of the portion of
treasure I had brought, left for now in Tlachta's care. A better
place than that would have to be found for it. "Do you want to
put on dry clothes, and I will take care of your wet things? There
is food for you when you are ready."

I changed gratefully and did the best I could with my wet hair.
Already I missed Roisin's help. By the time I was done, the serving
girl was back. But I asked her to wait a moment, while I freed
Fintan from the wicker cage he had sheltered in through the storm,
and watched while he hopped out to explore his new home.

We ate soup and bread, and Roisin was full of chatter, wanting
to know if my chamber was all right (I assured her it was) and
was my bed made up (it wasn't, but I lied and said yes, figuring

I would have to start doing without her soon enough) and had I seen the marvelous device they had for drying clothes? I hadn't, but I found it hard to concentrate on her description of the tiny stone building that was heated with a constant turf-fire and filled with drying racks. I was nervous, wondering what was to come. Surely there was more to starting an apprenticeship than claiming a bed? I looked to Geanann and found his eyes already resting upon me. With a smile, he nodded to the door.

It was Tlachta, her timing (as always, I have learned) perfect.

"You are dry and fed, now? Good. Well then, Luaine, we had best get started. Will you come with me?" And off she went, leaving me to trail after her like a child.

Ξ

Well, Cathbad had taught me to endure a druid's stare, but with Tlachta it was a whole new experience. For once all self-consciousness about my scar dropped away, for in her eyes it was invisible. It was my heart she was seeking, and as I sat across from her and ordered myself to keep still under her gaze, I understood that she had as little interest in my name and my holdings as she did in my good looks. In this place, such things did not matter.

After a long moment, with a tiny nod and an even tinier smile, she released me. Odd, that feeling. She looked at me still, but the sensation of being searched was gone.

"I understand your life has not been an easy one of late." This time the smile was warmer. "Know that you are welcome to stay with us on the island for as long as you have need." Her hand rose, forestalling any reply.

"However, I am told you wish to become an initiate. Is this correct?"

"Yes, mistress."

Who told her, I wondered. Geanann? But she had been waiting for us. Unless he had sent a message that somehow arrived faster than we could travel. Or… I shivered at the thought. Had she known I was coming before I myself did?

"You come highly recommended," Tlachta continued. "But, you understand, I must be satisfied myself that an initiate is suitable."

"Of course, mistress." There would be a test, then. I tried to remain calm, while my stomach began to jump around as it had when Eirnin used to grill me in my lessons. It was long since I had studied anything but my own survival. I was not sure what I remembered.

"Good. Then let's see what you have learned so far."

She began with the simple triads from my earliest lessons.

"Name the three divisions of the world."

"Earth, sea and air."

"The three divisions of nature."

"Animal, vegetable and mineral."

"The three divisions of man."

"Body, soul and spirit."

By the time we moved on to more complex questions—the eight winds, the seven divisions of the firmament, the truths of the poet, the duties of the king—I was more confident, and I could feel my studies coming back to me. The knowledge was all there, after all, locked away and waiting to be called back to my head.

She took her time, leading me through the landscape of all I had learned. From the names of the constellations to the names of Ulster's kings, from the mysterious triple face of the Morrigu to the familiar geography of Muirthemne, Tlachta took the sounding of my mind. By the time I finished reciting one of Lasair's battle sagas, she knew as much about my education as my own teachers.

Tlachta turned to a great chest that lay against the wall and brought out an armful of yew wands. I could see the white notches cut against the rich red of the polished wood. She laid the bundle before me and fanned it open, for the sticks were drilled with holes and attached together at the bottom.

"Do you know what these are?"

"Yes, mistress. It is Ogham writing."

"Can you read it?"

"Yes…but I have never seen the wands bound together so."

"Ah. Tell me then: Why do you think they are bound?"

I was too curious to be nervous and this freed me to think. "It must be to keep the wands in order," I offered. "The messages on the wands must be sequential."

"Good. Will you read some for me?"

It was a simple memorial—the name of a king and his death date and the name of his father. The next wand held the name of another king, the son of the first man, with again his death date and ancestry. And so it continued.

"It is the genealogy of the kings of Leinster," she explained, "kept in the order of their reigns. There are six bundles, recording the lives of some thirty kings. We have other bundles that document contracts undertaken at the Samhain judgments. We set them down in case of future disputes."

I was a little puzzled by that. I had studied some law, but only as it applied to everyday householding: the exchange price of livestock, recompense for property damage, the obligations of fostering and so on. Nobody would bother recording such agreements; in a dispute, the judgment and witness of a druid, or even the local chieftain or king, would be more than enough.

Tlachta was speaking of another level of judgment altogether. I realized suddenly that my conception of law had been too narrow—that judgments and contracts might draw borders and define kingdoms, save lives or lose them, bind or be broken by generations to come.

She must have sensed my interest, for she interrupted my testing to say something that has echoed in my mind ever since.

"Luaine, what does the law say if a free man is killed by another, say in a drunken brawl?"

A simple question. "His family must pay the dead man's family his honor price."

"Correct. And when your father was killed in battle, it is a rather different recompense was taken, was it not?"

Conall Cearnach, laying out his row of bloody heads for my mother. They had filled me with weary sorrow, but my mother had been glad to see my father properly avenged.

"The rule of war is different," I protested.

"The rule of war is different," she agreed. "Should, then, kings and chieftains be free to set the men of Ireland against each other for squabbles over cattle or women, and will our warriors forever spill each other's blood for the sake of insults and rivalries? Do they live free from any law but their own code?"

I had no reply to her words. They disturbed and excited me both, for I saw the truth in what she said and yet...a saying flashed into my mind: A tame wolf is merely a dog. Was not the same true of a warrior?

Tlachta's gaze was on the peat fire now, her voice soft and private. "If Ireland's rivers run red with the blood of her own warriors, who will be left to defend us when invaders land on our shores? There are men across the sea hungry for conquest: yellow-haired warriors in long ships, and an army from the hot lands so vast that it consumes its neighbors as a fire consumes thatch."

Then her eyes were on me, so intense they seemed to glow yellow in the dim light. "The druids have foreseen this," she said, and the hair stood up on my arms for I hadn't the least doubt that what she said was true. "It is time for the tribes of Ireland to unite under their high king and to be bound to a common law."

There are many branches of study to explore in the druid's long training. But I believe I was called to the Law on my very first day, when Tlachta gave me a vision of a world in which sworn brothers need not fight each other on the whim of a queen, nor a man slay his own son over a withheld name.

Ξ

The day was wearing to a close, but Tlachta had not finished with me. For, as she explained, "You have excellent recall and an inquiring mind, and these are both important. But an initiate must also have the potential to learn in another way. It is the druid's task to see what is hidden, to hear what is unsaid. It is the truth that lies beneath the surface of the world that we seek."

I knew what she spoke of, knew too, that I had that ability. Whether I would ever be at ease with it was another question.

She must have seen my discomfort. "Will you walk with me?" she asked. "We will go to the tip of the island. These things are easier to speak of there."

The farther we walked along the shoreline, the more the magic of the island took hold. My slightly disappointing first impression that this long finger of land was an "ordinary" settlement faded as we left first the buildings and then the fields behind. As we walked along the strip of sand that edged the island, the sounds of human life were replaced with birdcalls. The reedy shoreline bustled with waterbirds: plovers, yellowlegs, gray herons and jet-black coots. And with every step, the wild calling in the air grew louder.

When we reached the tip of the island, I caught my breath. Now, I realized, I saw the place of deep mystery that was the Isle of Women. It was not back at the settlement. It was not even on this lonely tip of land, silent and still but for the raucous cries overhead.

Past the reeds, across a narrow channel of still gray water, lay a second island. It spread before us, flat and green, the air above it snowy with untold numbers of wheeling, shrieking terns. They sliced the air above our heads, white and black spears of flight, but always they returned to the far shore.

From the dead center of the island loomed an ancient evergreen tree, massive and black. The trunk of it thrust from the earth like a mountain—it would take three or four people, I guessed, to span its girth—and its bottom branches brushed the ground, nearly as long as the tree was tall.

Tlachta let me gaze at the sight in silence for some time. Then she motioned me to a bench that faced out across the water.

"Do you know what kind of tree that is?"

I knew. The shape suggested it, but I did not guess. I knew.

"It is a yew."

"The terns nest on that island. They will leave sometime after

Samhain, but always they return in the spring. They are beloved of Mug Ruith, for they are masters of the air and they greet his rising with loud cries and exuberant feats."

I smiled at the thought, but it was the yew that filled my vision.

"The yew tree has been there for as long as human memory stretches back," Tlachta said. "It is a tree of sanctuary and renewal, for the living and for the dead. Its roots sink deep, even to the Otherworld, while its branches stretch up to the sun god's light."

I had seen others, of course, at sacred places; yews marked springs and groves and graves all over the country. Now I understood why.

"You feel the power of the place, do you not?" she asked.

I nodded without breaking my gaze. The dark tree called to me. It was both frightening and comforting. Don't ask me how that can be. It is a thing not to be understood until it is experienced. "Yes, I feel it." My voice was soft as a sigh.

"Tell me, then. Has it ever happened that you felt such a thing before? Known or seen something that others don't?"

Oh, yes. Only I did not like to speak of most of them. I began with the easiest to tell: the way I had recognized Liban, the woman of the Sidhe, when she came to my father's side at Samhain, and the time when Fintan's feather showed me the ships sailing into our bay.

"Cathbad taught you to use a Messenger?"

Her interruption was sharp—sharp enough that I tore my eyes from the island to search her face. Was she angry? There was consternation there, certainly.

"No, Mistress. He only gave Fintan to me for a companion, and bade me care for him. I…" I stopped myself. I had been about to say "I taught myself," but that did not feel right.

"It was Fintan taught me." It was as close to the truth as I could get.

"I see." Tlachta smiled at me. "And I see also why Cathbad thinks you a promising candidate." Hazel eyes held mine, considering.

"There is more, isn't there?"

I sighed. In truth, this conversation, though it had sealed my acceptance to the isle, had made me question my fitness for it. I was not sure I wanted to open the door to more visions. I saw no reasonable response but honesty.

"I have seen things, Mistress, that I would rather not see."

Haltingly, I told her what had happened to me at my coming of age, when I watched my father's Gae Bolga kill a young man I knew to be my brother. Tlachta's grave face was still through the telling, and she did not move even when my eyes spilled over with tears at the memory. Only when I fell silent and my breath calmed, did she speak.

"It is difficult when such strong visions come upon a child with no training," she said. "There is little wonder you found them overwhelming and frightening. Will you trust me when I tell you that with time and study, you will learn to be at ease with this gift? I will not say there will be no horror or pain in it—not so long as pain is a part of life. Did your father not suffer on that day, also, though his vision failed him?"

I let my eyes travel the smooth green body of the island and then up to the wheeling white flecks that danced about it, and I thought about her words. I did not completely understand them, but I nearly did, and I found it was enough.

"I do trust you," I said at last. "And I am ready to learn what you have to teach me."

Besides, I had discovered something about myself, a secret nestled perhaps in the stiff black arms of the yew or chiming softly amidst the bird cries. I had lied to Tlachta—or rather to myself—when I said that I would rather not have my visions. When I looked deep inside and asked would I truly give up the Sight that I shared with Fintan, would I rather see only what everyone saw—the honest answer was no.

I had a hunger for the truth, you see. And the truth does not come without cost.

CHAPTER 22
SAMHAIN ON THE ISLAND

By midday my friends were gone, and I was alone among strangers.

Geanann left first, and it would not surprise me if he planned it so as not to overshadow my parting from Roisin. He is like that.

I had already chosen what to give Berach and Roisin: a set of matched gold torcs, richer than was really suited to their rank. But they would look splendid on their wedding day, and if they never wore them again they would at least have some treasure that could be traded at need. Geanann was harder. No gift could repay what he had given me.

I said as much as I handed him the enameled cloak pin.

It was too small, I realized in dismay. The rich objects I had reached for at first—jeweled goblets, golden armbands—had all seemed to me to underline the impossible gap between the gift of a life and any mere treasure, but now I was afraid that I would seem mean or ungrateful.

"It is only a token," I explained, "and if there are gold or gems in my cache that your eye favors, you have only to choose. But this I chose, for it has a special meaning to me. It marks the first time Fintan showed me how to look through his eyes, the day I saw the ships sailing to Baile's Strand." And I told him how my father had won that pin from Baire in a game of fidchell the time Baire was camped on our strand, and how he had given it to me—even though it was sized for a man's cloak—because it was cunningly fashioned as a raven.

"So," I concluded, "you could say that Fintan was my first guide along this path. And you were the second."

I dared look at him then, and all my hesitation fell away when I saw how his face lit up with pleasure at my story.

"It has been an honor to be your guide for this short time," Geanann told me, and he took out his old pin and replaced it with mine, skewering the raven's beak through the circle of its body. He stepped forward then, placed his hands on my shoulders and kissed the top of my head in blessing.

"I will check in on you when my travels bring me south again," he promised. "But now my father awaits my report, and it has been too many months since my master in the healing arts has had sight of me."

"Will he be angry that you were delayed looking after me?"

He shook his head. "He will be pleased that I have put my training to good use and eager to hear of my first treatment with the poppy."

And so we parted good friends.

Roisin, though. Here was a thing I had not foreseen: that parting from her would feel like losing the last of my family, and that the loneliness filling me as I watched her ride down the lane would raise, like the cold currents that sweep up from the hidden depths of the sea, all the grief and fear that had gripped me when my mother died.

We clung to each other's necks and shed tears at our good-byes, but I hope she did not guess how I had to force myself to let her go.

"Tara is not so far," I managed at last. "Not for seasoned travelers like us. And I am told my mistress presides over the Samhain rites on a great hill not far from Tara. I won't lose track of you."

"You had best not or you will face my wrath, which is a more fearsome thing altogether than any warrior," she replied, regaining her tart humor even through her tears. I might not have held myself together, without that. Then her face grew earnest. "I am counting on you to give the blessing to our babies."

And so they were gone, and I could not stay my weeping. But it was not the desolation of death that returned with Roisin's parting, but only its echo. I spent half the afternoon with Fintan, walking the island's tip, and Tlachta must have told the others to let me be, for I was not disturbed. And as the turmoil in my heart calmed, the understanding came to me that the web that had brought Roisin and me together was not ruptured, but only expanded. Our paths would intersect again.

Nor was I alone—not for long, not surrounded as I was with women. Some, surely, would in time become my friends. I was ready, now, to meet them.

Ξ

Life at the Isle of Women was different from anything I had known, but within a few days I was more at home than I had ever been at Emain Macha. My fear—that the close quarters and tight boundaries of the island would be suffocating—proved unfounded.

For one thing, Tlachta ensures that our privacy is respected. Both the work of memorization and the growth of the inner eye require solitude, and despite the intensity of our training I can always find time to be alone. I don't think I have ever taken a

walk with Fintan that I didn't pass others—pacing the beach or
sitting silently under a tree—but we never speak or disturb each
other at such times.

But the other thing, the thing that is harder to explain, is that
the island seems larger than it is. Though I rarely leave it, I do not
feel confined. Perhaps it is because the island rests so close to the
Otherworld that it seems to expand at need and to present new
features and vistas even on the most familiar paths. And then of
course there is the other island—what I have come to think of as
the *real* island. We do not name it, for it is a world unto itself.

When I first came here, there were only two other apprentices
in their first year of study. We soon knew each other well, for
we spent many hours of every day together. Bronach was the
youngest of us, only twelve and by the looks of her not yet a
woman. Dark, skinny and silent, she radiated a brooding intensity
that was truly a little frightening. I imagined her family sending
her here with some relief, not knowing what on earth else to do
with such a girl.

And then there was poor Muireann. Or perhaps I should not
say poor, for she seems happy enough now. She was sixteen when
I arrived and had already been at the island for two years. She
came seeking refuge from a vicious father, and at first helped in
the kitchen and with the herb preparation. And from there, I
suppose, it was not a far jump to wishing she might take up the
training herself. It was apparent to me within weeks, though, that
Muireann could not keep up. As the moons waxed and waned, she
fell farther and farther behind. Her pretty face became drawn, and
at night I sometimes heard her weeping quietly in the dark. Before
it came time for her to take the formal vows that transform an

SERC LIBRARY

initiate to a full apprentice, Muireann went to Tlachta and asked to be released from her training. She has not left us, though. She works still with the herbals, and has also begun helping with the trading and provisioning. Perhaps she will spend her life here; for though she is golden-haired and plump-cheeked, she says she has no wish for any husband of her own.

There was a gap of several years to the next newest apprentices, a group of about ten who were all halfway or better to earning the white robe that marks a first-degree druid. Another four or five were, like Geanann, working toward their second degree, using the isle as a home base but leaving freely to lend their services or to study with a master adept in their specialization. It takes fourteen years of study to attain the feathered robe, and along with it the right to perform any of the druids' offices, save only taking apprentices of their own, acting as chief druid to a king, or performing the Bull Feast to choose a high king. These only the tonsured masters may undertake.

Do you imagine me reading omens into bird flights, inducing visions and conducting secret, sacred rites? Then I will tell you now—the first year of a druid's apprenticeship is a dull, never-ending stream of straight memorization, punctuated with menial physical tasks like grinding herbs, preparing and laying wood for ceremonial fires and cleaning away the smelly remains from sacrifices or divination. There is little of the discussion and explanation I anticipated, not even as much as in Cathbad's classes, and virtually none of the druid's secret knowledge. And the work is relentless.

Day after day, we were simply, ruthlessly, stuffed with words—verse after verse of them, history upon history, classifications, genealogies, impenetrable triads, medicinal recipes, legal tracts. I was kept awake at night by the gibbering fragments of lists and lore chasing about in my head, and when at last I slept, my dreams more often than not trapped me in failed recitations and lectures spoken in some incomprehensible tongue.

It was another test, of course. It was Saraid, who sleeps with her two young children in the bed next to mine, who told me. I had wakened her with my dreaming, yelling apparently that there was no corner of space left in my head and they must leave off lest it burst open. "It will get better," she whispered to me in the dark. "They weed out the weak plants as early as possible. If you endure through the first year, then they know you have the strength to continue."

"Next year will be easier, then?" I asked.

"I did not say easier."

$$\equiv$$

I have not mentioned our teachers. Besides Tlachta, there is one other druid master on the isle. Her name is Macha. She is old and very fat, with a wheezy chest and thin white hair that sprouts unevenly from the line of her tonsure. Macha teaches us everything to do with the history of Ireland—its origins and invasions and battles and people—and while her frail voice sometimes gives out, her mind never does, but is as precise and nimble as a cat. Her knowledge of astronomy is also great—but she leaves that to others now, for the night air is cruel to her old bones.

Of the others, my favorite teacher is Rathnait. Her passion is the earth and its vast lore, and she says its lessons must be read with the body as well as the mind. So even in our first year, she would sometimes relieve us of the endless memory work and lead us out to forage for herbs or read weather in the clouds. It was like a release from captivity, these little excursions, and I returned with a new sense of space in my overcrowded head.

Tlachta herself we see little of, for she works mainly with the more advanced apprentices. She is wise not only in law, but in ceremonial magic, ritual, divination and sacrifice. It is for this knowledge that she leads the Samhain ceremony for the high king himself.

I had not been long at my studies when the autumn wind grew cold teeth and the wheel of the sun left the sky earlier each day. I had no doubt that Samhain on the island would be unlike any I had known.

Tlachta would not be there. The daughter of Mug Ruith makes the long journey each year to preside over Tara's Samhain ceremonies, and the hill where the great fire is lit is now called the Hill of Tlachta. There are hills closer to Tara that might be more convenient for the high king, but there is none in all Ireland so close to the Otherworld. My mistress and her helpers spend more than a week there every year, seeing to the preparations and presiding over the judgments afterward.

Those of us who remained on the Isle of Women had no hill, but then we did not need our fire to be seen far and wide, but only by our own little community. I knew where our Samhain bonfire would be—by the yew tree, at the heart of the island's power.

Ξ

Tlachta made it clear before she left that the first-year students were not to invite visions or have any contact with the Sidhe. "Some of the senior apprentices will be seeking dreams of power," she said. "You are not to join in their rituals or drink the dream draught. If you see people of the Sidhe or spirits of the dead, do not speak to them. Simply look away, and let them pass by. If you are frightened in any way, seek out Macha. She can protect you."

And so we were put to work as Samhain laborers. As a child, I had always marveled at how the Samhain fire lit without fail, even in the foulest weather. It is not, I hope, giving away too much of the druid's craft if I reveal that this has less to do with magic than with painstaking preparation. Every single log that goes into the Samhain fire has been soaked in oil or rolled in fat ahead of time. It is backbreaking work that leaves a person greasy and rank as a rendering floor.

But we were bathed and clean as evening fell and we paddled our way back by threes and fours in our little coracles to the dark shores of the island. And in the black of night before the fire was lit, as the songs and chants were offered, I felt them before I saw them—the Other ones, exhaled on the island's misty breath, drifting across its waters. The veil that held them back was thin here at any time; on Samhain it simply wafted away like smoke and our worlds mingled. I watched in wonder as the fire leapt up, revealing tall men and women with silver hair and jeweled gowns holding their hands out to its warmth. As the night wore on I saw many of them stop to converse with one or other of our women, sometimes at length and earnestly. Indeed I am sure I saw Treasa, who will win her feathered cloak next season, entwined in a shining figure's arms, her face lifted up to his kiss, as they vanished together into the darkness. Others of our women lay in a dream trance, their eyes faraway, mouths moving without sound. I remembered my instructions, though, and if the eyes of one of our visitors fell upon me, I would nod respectfully and look away, and they would drift by without stopping.

And so the night passed until nearly dawn. I was tired by then, my shoulders achy from hauling wood and my eyes worn out, it seemed, from the wonders parading before them. I hunkered into my cloak, dropped my head onto my knees and let my eyelids close.

I felt her presence, as surely as I had in the Speckled House so long ago. She hovered before me, not passing by as the others had, and finally I raised my head, thinking perhaps she waited for the polite acknowledgment I had given the others.

It was Liban. I knew her, and she knew me also and had waited to speak with me. Knowing this—that she remembered the young girl who had been a mere bystander to the drama that played out the night she came to my father's sickbed—I could not look away. I rose to my feet and bowed my head to her, and when she smiled I remembered the first smile she had given me, and I but a child of eight summers.

"I have come this night to speak with you," she said, "and though I have seen you avoid others of my kind, it is my hope you will remember me and know I bring no harm."

"I remember you, lady," I said. "It is honored I am by your presence."

She grew serious then. "I have come to tell you I am sorry for the death of Cuchulainn, a hero well-deserving of my sister's love, and of Emer too, who was a woman of great heart. For when news came to us of this grievous loss, my sister Fand sent up a lament for her lover of old. But I thought of you, Luaine, left on this earth alone, and I remembered how your eyes knew me even as a child. So it is glad, but not surprised, I am to find you here, though,"—and here her silvery outline leaned in toward me as she looked more closely—"I see there has been harm done along the way, after all."

There was anger in her voice then, and I was so moved by her concern that for a moment my throat threatened to close off my words. But I found them again. When there is need, the words come.

"There was harm done," I agreed, "but it has been healed, and I am well."

Long fingers reached toward me, and I was startled to feel them warm and solid against my cheek. I suppose I expected her to dissolve against me like a misty illusion. In fact the warmth became a heat, radiating into my scar, and my eyes widened at the sensation.

Finally she drew back her hand. "There is a little more healing for you, such as I can offer," she said. "But why I have come is to give you this." She placed in my hand a crystal teardrop. I could feel its many facets against my palm. "If there is ever a time you have need of me, hold this in the sun's rays, or even against the fire or lamp's flame, until it breaks the light into a fan of colors. Call my name, and I will come through the rainbow light. For your father served us well against our enemies when he came to the Happy Plain, and his memory is honored among us."

I gazed at her in astonishment and stammered out my thanks. Before my eyes she began to drift back and grow dim, until finally she was truly no more than the mist I had imagined.

The next morning I looked in a mirror, hoping that Liban had somehow erased the mark of my wound. She had not, but her touch was healing nonetheless, for the scar has never again kept me awake with its aching. When the weather makes it grumble, it is not long before a steady soothing heat grows within it, and the pain quiets.

CHAPTER 23
THE WHITE BLOSSOM

I had but one visit from Geanann that first year, for he would be eligible for the feathered robe in just over a year's time, and his two masters were pushing him hard.

"Fingin is determined I shall have the skill of the god of healing himself before he is done with me, while my father will allow no scrap of knowledge from the other branches of learning to be overlooked," he told me ruefully. "It is all I can do to survive their zeal."

"You are at Emain, then," I said, my voice flat. Fingin was Conchobor's personal healer. It sickened me to think of Geanann there, right under the king's nose. Foolish, I know. There was no healer more renowned than Fingin. Who else would Geanann study under?

But I was surprised to see him shaking his head. "I will not stay there," he said, his eyes dark and hard. "I am with my mother's people, not far west of Emain. There is travel back and forth, of course, but I prefer that. My father knows the reason. Fingin does not, but he accepts it." Then he flashed me a quick smile. "Actually, Fingin probably does know something of the reason. There is little that escapes him. But he has a physician's discretion."

We talked of lighter things, then, and the hours flew by until the time came for his leaving. And then he laid his hand on my shoulder and returned to the subject of the king.

"I began my apprenticeship when I was only twelve years old," he said to me. I did the figuring in my head—he was twenty-five, then. Ten years older than me. "It is half my life I have been on this path, and now my goal is within my sight. I cannot change masters now, not so close to my testing."

I would not ask or expect it, I began to say, but I remembered how my heart had gone cold at the thought of him there, and realized I had indeed, in some secret place, hoped for it. So I did not say a half-truth, but only nodded my understanding.

"But it is this I wish for you to know, Luaine. I am not bound to Conchobor, nor will I be. When I win my robe, I will be gone from that place, and Conchobor no more aware of my absence than he is of my presence now. To him, I am just one of Cathbad's many apprentices."

I was not sure he was right about that. Conchobor did not get where he was by being oblivious to his surroundings, and I didn't imagine the identity of Cathbad's son escaped him. But I was glad Geanann would not stay with Conchobor. It was selfish of me, perhaps, to put my own grudge before Geanann's prospects, for there is no doubt he could become the king's physician after Fingin. But I was glad all the same.

Ξ

I had messages from Roisin that year too, so I knew that King Lugaid had indeed remembered Berach and welcomed him into his service. But it was not until the following Samhain that I was able to see her.

Late in the summer, Tlachta called me to the small cluttered room where she had first interviewed me and made her proposal.

"I do not usually invite the less experienced apprentices to assist me at Samhain," she said. I had taken my vows the week before and was now a "true" apprentice. "However, you have proved to me the seriousness of your calling, and I believe you may take a special interest in observing the judgments in the days that follow. Also,"—and here her lips twitched into a rare smile—"I am aware that you have dear friends in the area. I'm sure we could manage to free you for a visit."

I needed no persuading. But Tlachta had not finished with me. This journey, she explained, brought to urgency a problem she had been mulling over for some time.

"You do not strike me as a person who will wish to spend her life hidden away on the Isle of Women," she said to me. "Yet if you leave these shores, how long will it be until word reaches Conchobor of a young woman of the same name and age as his wife, her face blemished as though by a poet's curse? And given such news, how long will he believe in your death, which was never proved?"

"I have worried about this also," I confessed. "I suppose I thought that I would be here for some years, and that…well, that the king was not likely to live a great deal longer."

Tlachta had none of my squeamishness in anticipating another's death.

"You could wait for him to die," she agreed frankly. "But Conchobor has been a strong man all his life. Despite his age, he may have a good many years left to him."

I was trapped, then. Except…I glanced up quickly. Tlachta's hazel eyes, tinged gold in their intensity, were trained on me like a hawk's.

"You have a plan," I said. "You would not have invited me to the Hill of Tlachta if you did not. What am I to do?"

She leaned forward, her eyes never leaving my own.

"You must leave Luaine behind and become another," she said. "You must dream for a name."

Ξ

I had wondered how I would ever manage to sleep. To seek a true dream, I was to sleep on the wattles of knowledge. And while the very name filled me with awe, the reality—a lumpy rack of woven rowan whips erected under the great yew tree—looked very uncomfortable indeed.

But the dream draught is powerful, and so is the body's demand for rest after the long vigil that precedes a dreaming. Indeed, as I lowered myself gingerly onto the wattle bed, I realized it did not matter if I even closed my eyes. I had been two nights without sleep, and fatigue had made my waking into a series of fragmented, brightly colored episodes as strange as dreaming. If there was a vision meant for me, it would find me.

The stars wheeled overhead like an endless tapestry recounting the deeds of a strange world, framed at one corner of my vision by a black fringe of yew branches. The bright patterns coalesced and scattered before me, so that at one moment my eyes beheld a familiar constellation, or a fanciful picture of my own invention—a warrior's steed, a handled mirror—and the next nothing but a random infinity of light. And then it was as if a heavy black cloak was drawn over the sky, and the stars became darkness, and I slept.

The lawn is studded with stars. No…I see now, not stars at all, but the tiny white flowers that used to nestle in the grass around our house in the spring. There is no sign of a house, though, nor any familiar landmark to say where I might be.

Movement catches my eye—it is a seedling, pushing out of the grass and into the sky. Another grows beside it, and both of them stretching up and unfolding leaves so fast that in the space of several breaths they have become young saplings: a sturdy straight oak tree and a graceful white-skinned birch. They reach to the sky, and as they swell in girth the two trunks first touch and then grow together so that they form one inseparable column and their branches intertwine and mingle in the sky. And neither beauty nor strength are lost, for the oak grows straight and true, and the birch branches dance lightly in the wind, and each is a perfect specimen of its kind. Together they are a marvel.

Then the skies darken. Heavy clouds cloak the sun, rain beats down on the oak leaves and wind lashes the delicate birch branches. But the two trees stand proud and strong and pay as little mind to the weather's violence as they do to a passing breeze. The winds cannot touch them.

But they are not unassailable. Even as a sudden foreboding grips me, there is a rumbling in the sky. The white fire forks out of the clouds. My head swims with the crack of it, and for a heartbeat, two, my eyes see only darkness punctuated with jagged phantom flares of light. The strange burnt smell hurts my nostrils.

I know what I will see when my vision clears. The two trees are cloven to the roots, felled to the ground with a single stroke. Smoking, writhing, they darken to black and crumble away.

Such desolation. I want to turn away, but I can't. I am compelled to watch until the last blackened twig collapses into ash and earth. And it is because I cannot turn away that I see the tiny green shoot that trembles into life. Slow and fragile at first, it sprouts from the very place where the two great trunks were sundered. The sun kisses it, and now it brightens to a dark and glossy green, leaves unfurling proudly, leaping up to the light. Strong, shapely, it is a plant I have never seen. Its upward rush slows, stops, and from the topmost branch the hard bump of a bud appears. Swelling and lengthening, the bud bursts into glorious bloom. White, luminously white, its beauty shines in that dark place and banishes despair.

I awoke at the first thin light of dawn, shivering in the chill dampness, dew heavy on my hair and blanket and the imprint of the woven rowan branches engraved painfully into my skin. The dream's grip was still upon me, so that I felt I was only half in this world. It was an exhilaration in my blood, for I knew it was a dream of power. I had not been given a name, but I had been given something. I rushed to the little boat pulled up on the shore and started across the water. I must speak to Tlachta before the dream faded.

≡

"But it is your name, plainly."

I shook my head. "Mistress, there were no words at all in my dream. I heard no name."

Tlachta looked at me sharply. "You have a bright mind, Luaine, and are keen in understanding. Do not tell me you have not seen in the oak and birch trees your own peerless parents, their rise and fall?"

"I did think of it," I admitted.

"Well, then."

She was not making this easy for me.

"Well, I suppose then that the plant that rose from their ashes could be me." Or the legend that lives on after a great life, or Ulster itself, which my father gave his life for, or King Lugaid whom he trained, I thought. It seemed presumptuous to push myself into that place.

"Of course it is you. Are you not their offspring, and did you not come close to your own death at that time and rise back up into life?"

She rose then, and bade me kneel before her. Macha and Rathnait rose and stood on either side of Tlachta as she laid both hands on my head. They gave a long prayer of greeting, inviting all beings—those of our world and those of the worlds beyond—to bear witness to their words. And then Tlachta said in a loud voice, "I name you Finscoth. Let you be known by this name henceforth, and may you live true to the course this name sets for you."

White Blossom. I knelt and kept silent, struggling within myself to accept Tlachta's words. I understood the charge she put on me: to cultivate that flower in my heart, to strive for a soul as luminous and pure as my dream. Yet my cheeks burned when I pictured the years to come. No one who met me would be thinking of the flower of my soul. They would be thinking, with amusement or pity or scorn, of the inescapable contrast between my name and my face. It was a name for a great beauty. I did not think I would ever feel it my own.

"It is your true name," Tlachta told me, when the ceremony was over and we were alone. "You have only to believe it to make it so."

I tried to believe, as I made my way to breakfast. It was my first proper meal in two days, and I had been ravenous when I awoke. But the thought of announcing my new name to all those women made my stomach buzz and jump. I would have a hard time eating.

CHAPTER 24
THE HILL OF TLACHTA

Tara is the sacred jewel in the territory of the high king, a territory that borders each of the four provinces and thus gathers all of Ireland to itself. It is, in fact, a good deal closer to Muirthemne than to the Isle of Women. And so I found myself, sooner than I could have foreseen, journeying north toward my homeland.

We traveled in comfort this time, by main roads and well protected. Chieftains were honored to lodge us, and the weather held crisp and clear. Orlagh was frisky as we set out, dancing through the drifts of leaves, and my heart was as glad as hers. But I awoke on the second morning of our travels with my high spirits of the previous day vanished. At first it was just a vague uneasiness that I put down to restless sleep, but hour by hour, mile by mile, a foreboding grew that I could not shake. Though I told myself it was only my own nervousness at this first venturing out of the protection of the island, by nightfall I knew it was something more. I ate my supper in near silence, unable to enjoy the lively banter of our host's table, wondering what, if anything, I should do about the shadow that had settled over my mind.

It was a relief when Tlachta asked to speak with me. I was hovering at the edge of asking her counsel, held back by my reluctance to burden her when she had already so much to see to.

There was no privacy to be had—not unless we braved the night chill—but we found a low space under the eaves, far from the fire and the conversation, and settled ourselves on the cold flagstone floor. Tlachta was direct, as always.

"How are you feeling, Finscoth?" The name was so new I hardly recognized it as my own.

Once, perhaps, I would have felt foolish confessing such vague fears. I had learned better. If Tlachta thought my feelings worth discussing, then they were worth discussing.

"It is uneasy I am, Mistress, without knowing why. The feeling has grown on me all this day. In truth, I can think of little else."

Tlachta nodded. "I, too, sense some darkness ahead. I thought it concerned you in some way. Now I am sure of it."

A flicker of panic licked at me. I was remembering the other times, the times the black hand had squeezed at my innards and the message its dark fingers had delivered. Someone is dead, I thought. Roisin. Berach. Maybe the high king himself. Lugh save me, what has happened?

I must have spoken that last part aloud, for Tlachta raised an eyebrow at my appeal to my father's patron, Lugh of the Long Hand. He is a sun god too, of course, and with a greater name than Mug Ruith. To this day he is closer to my heart than the god of our island, for he is the god who shone on my childhood.

That single eyebrow was enough to check my runaway fears, and Tlachta's next words brought them under rein.

"Stop now. It is not a time to let wild imaginings take hold. Let us see what can be learned from this message."

She questioned me for some time: What, exactly, did the foreboding feel like? It was the first time I had ever described the black fingers to another person, and though my words were halting and unsure I could see she understood me.

"And is it the same this time as it was before, when your brother was killed or when you foresaw Deirdriu's death?"

This brought me up short. It was not the same, was it? Or only in general type (the scrabbly feeling in my guts, the uneasiness, the sense of shadow) but not at all in its particulars. My vision of Deirdriu had made me cry out in fear and sorrow; my certainty that the youth of Ulster would be killed had squeezed my heart with grief. And in the sacred grove, when I saw Conlaoch killed, the horror had been a black vise that all but crushed me.

"No, Mistress," I told Tlachta. "This is not the same. It is milder. And it does not fill me with grief."

She was nodding. "Now you are learning to look at these things head on. And what you describe matches my own foreboding, though it comes to me in a different manner. Now, let these feelings take hold of you, and answer me this: Do you still think something has happened?"

I took a deep breath, closed my eyes and surrendered to the shadow that had been tugging at my mind all day. I let it take me, unpleasant as it was, but I tried to keep one part of myself apart, to listen and watch. I felt it all, yet I could observe it too.

I opened my eyes. Tlachta waited patiently.

"No." I was sure of it.

"Then what do you think the feeling means?"

"It is a warning. I think it is a warning. And…" I hesitated, took a deep breath, plunged on. I was so new at this, so likely to be wrong. But Tlachta knew this. She asked only for my best try. "I do not think it is an omen of death. I think…I think there is danger for me at Tara."

Tlachta was silent, considering. Then she found one last question for me.

"Finscoth, may I borrow your Messenger?"

☰

If Cathbad had been at Tara, I could have sent Fintan with a more useful question. As it was, we had to send him to one of Lugaid's druids, who would have no knowledge of me or my history. It was Tlachta's message Fin carried, as she at least was known to the druids there, and knew where to direct him.

The question, though. We could come up with nothing more specific than, "Is all well at Tara?" If Tara was under attack, or in the grip of a plague, we would find out. But I doubted very much there was anything so dramatic amiss.

☰

"Do you wish to remain here, or go on? I'm sure our host will make you welcome, and we can pick you up on our return journey, if that seems best to you."

Fintan had left at first light and returned by midmorning. As expected, he had no alarming events to report. Now Tlachta, to my surprise, was leaving this decision to me. I had spent half the night mulling over the same question.

"If it is permitted, Mistress, I will go on. It might be wiser to stay, but I would discover what awaits me. And if my foreboding is indeed a message, then I am thinking the message is not to turn back, but rather to be cautious in my going forward."

I don't know where I got the nerve for such a speech. As if I had any business even interpreting such vaporous inklings. It was like trying to assign a shape to smoke. But I had my own reasons, and not only my eagerness to see Roisin, that propelled me. In the darkest hours of night, a kind of pugnacious determination had come over me. I had already lost my old life. But I had begun

again and I would not now be turned back from my new path.
I would go forward and meet my fate.

≡

We did not go into Tara, but straight to the Hill of Tlachta,
arriving mid-afternoon. Preparations for the Samhain were
already underway, and I was put to work, as the previous year,
hauling and greasing the wood. It felt odd at first to work side
by side with the male apprentices from Tara, but in a strange way
my scar made it easier. Because they were not interested in me as
a woman, we were more quickly comfortable as colleagues.

The fire here would be huge, half again as tall as a man, and
constructing it was a job that would take much of the next day.
And there were other preparations—the torches to bind and
soak, the altar to clean, the sacrificial tools to sharpen. The site
was open and smooth from long years of use, but patches of gorse
and thistle still sprang up each summer and had to be cleared.

After inspecting the site and assigning us our duties, Tlachta
and Rathnait rode on to Tara in the late afternoon. Evidently
the apprentices were to stay overnight, sleeping in the circle of
small tents that had been erected by the foot of the hill. I hoped
that one was set aside for Tlachta's women.

By the time we stopped to eat—long after the sun had gone
down—I was sweaty and redolent of pork grease and had worked
my jumpy feelings down to a quiet murmur. I wondered how
long it would take for us all to wash, sharing pots of hot water
heated over our campfire.

Ah, but there was no need. This was sacred ground and a
sacred ceremony, and all who assisted at the rites, however
humbly, were to come to Samhain thoroughly clean. They had

built a sweating house, a structure very like the little hot-air hut we had on the Isle of Women for drying clothing and herbs, but big enough for five or six people to go in at one time. I had heard of them, of course. Healers use them with fragrant herbs to ease labored breathing or old ones' joint pains, but I had never been inside one.

Myself and the two older female apprentices, being guests, went first. We scrubbed our greasy hands up to the shoulders with brushes and warm water, shucked off our clothes and entered the tiny building. The pit in the center was piled with hot stones, dragged from the core of the fire that burned beside the house. New stones had already been added to that fire, ready for the next group.

It was the hottest place I had ever been. So strange, it felt, to leave behind the chill nip of a late autumn night, stoop into a dark doorway, and have a wall of heat hit my face, solid and thick and almost suffocating. As soon as we found our places around the fire, the door was closed, and now the heat was black: an invisible all-surrounding presence. It seared my nose when I breathed, penetrated my lungs, heated my eyeballs. It was frightening at first, but as the heat seeped into my limbs, it became comfortable and finally, comforting. Sweat began to prick out on my skin—in my armpits and the crease of my neck, on my forehead and scalp. It was stinging and acrid at first—I could smell the other women too—but as the perspiration increased it ran clear as water. I was slick with it, even my hair, and I felt cleaner than ever in my life.

Damnhait, on my left, began chanting softly—a simple prayer that I had memorized mechanically as part of my training. Now,

in that dark place, it became luminous in my mind as we sang
it over and over.

Sky to the earth
Earth to the water
Water to the deep
Wings in the air
Legs on the earth
Fins under the waves
Night to day
The seasons turn
The firmament over all

The words, strung from one person to the next into a web of
meaning, released their power into the waiting darkness. We re-
created the wheel of the sun, the wheel of the seasons, the wheel
of life, and we turned as one with the wheel. For the first time, I
understood what prayer could do.

Afterward, we threw blankets over our shoulders and ran,
shrieking and giggling and splashing, into the little stream that
chattered behind the tents. Our hides were tingling pink and cold
when we clambered out, but our hosts had seen to our needs. We
found our clothes in a basket, waiting for us on the stream bank.

≡

My mother came to me in the night. She danced into my dream
on silent feet, so that it seemed to me I simply turned and there she
was. Emer was as beautiful as I remembered: hair a thick stream
of dark gold, a form both straight and shapely, eyes as green as
the silk of her dress.

It was the silk that kept me from rushing into her arms. Green as the barley fields in spring, it was. The same green that had wrapped my father's head. And as I gazed on it, my love for her turned sour in my breast. It was not hate I felt—hate would have been welcome, with its clean hot flame—but rather a bloated angry pain. *You abandoned me. You left me to face everything alone.*

I turned my back to her, shoulders hunching stiff against the pull of her presence, the poison of memory.

Yet there she stood again, in front of me, and though my face was turned away I saw all the same. The green eyes were sad and pleading. Her face was bright with love. Slowly, she compelled me to look full upon her. She raised her hands, cupped her palms together and breathed into the little bowl they formed. And then she offered it to me, a gift.

I looked into her hands, and I saw a birth. My birth. There was my mother, her hair dark with sweat, features tender and fierce, reaching for the tiny body that slipped out from between her legs, pushing away the midwife's hands to claim her baby girl. Then came a series of images that changed at a dizzying speed as Emer shuffled through her memories, deciding which to pick. Poignant glimpses of my childhood they were, but she hurried on. There was something more important she was looking for.

At last she opened her hands wide and showed me. There was Emer, speaking earnestly to Eirnin, determined to persuade him to teach me. Next I saw her standing against the fence during my arms lesson, watching Berach wallop me into the mud while she swallowed her worry and showed me only encouragement. Now I was walking out our gate onto the plain, with Fintan on my shoulder, and I saw my mother wave Tullia back and let me go unhindered. I saw her meet with one girl after another, and their families too, until finally choosing Roisin to be my maid. And at the last, I stood with my mother on a hill that looked like a reclining woman, memorizing the location of a treasure, and this time I could read her intent.

I understood. As Emer's hands closed, and the little worlds winked out, I looked on my mother and found the poison was gone. She had left me alone, but she had not left me unprepared.

I smiled at her. And as she faded back beyond the reach of dreams, her green eyes flashed at me, and her chin lifted in a gesture I suddenly realized was my own as well as hers. Her answering smile was full of pride—not for herself, but for me. My mother was proud of me.

Ξ

The blessing of that dream was short-lived, for I woke to a gray day and a mood to match. My jumpy stomach had returned while I slept, blown in, it seemed, on the wind that had risen in the night and the high, scudding clouds it chased across the sky.

Tlachta rode in from Tara around midday, bringing with her the answer to our mysterious fears. I could not believe her news.

"He is *here*? Now? But why?"

If she minded the way I lost my manners and fired questions at her as if she were a servant, she didn't show it. Tlachta is like that. She bends her mind to the problem at hand and shuts out all distractions. She was grim now, but focused. It would take much more than this—more than I can imagine, really—to throw her into a tizzy.

"Lugaid has summoned the rulers of the four provinces," she explained now, "and bid them attend Samhain at Tara. He asserts his rule and tests their allegiance."

"It is a test of trust, also," she added. "For they will have to leave their own chief druids behind, and perhaps others of their most trusted men, to conduct the Samhain rites and judgments in their own territories."

"And Conchobor has obeyed," I marveled. After years of standing against the rest of Ireland, I could not imagine he was eager to serve another's will.

A curt nod. "He has come at the high king's bidding, and left Cathbad and Sencha in charge at Emain Macha. He will be here, on this hill, by nightfall."

I am not by nature a flighty person, but at the first mention of Conchobor's arrival my heart had thudded in alarm and my head felt as though no air were reaching it. I was afraid of his very name. And with that thought I became angry and ashamed, enough to pull my thoughts together. *Calm. Control.* I set myself to be like my mistress, and began to see the thing for what it was.

"There is no reason," I said slowly, "that he and I should even cross paths, is there?" I was glad, now, for the plain brown cloaks the Samhain helpers wore, cloaks I would not have been caught dead in before my life changed. Saraid had laughed at my distaste when I first saw them. "They are not designed for beauty," she told me. "It is the rites themselves, and the Wise Ones conducting it, that the crowd should be watching, not us. If the helpers could be invisible, that would be best. As it is, we do our best to fade into the background." With the thick brown wool pulled over my head and shading my face, I would be nothing in Conchobor's eyes but an anonymous apprentice. For that matter, I could even stay in my tent for the night, though that would leave Tlachta short a hand.

"Not if we are careful," she agreed now. "You will keep your face shielded from the light of the flames, and you will do no task that brings you close to the men of Ulster. I will have Rathnait see to it.

"Conchobor will not, in any event, interrupt the Samhain," she said. "Should he come nose to nose with you, he will still wait until tomorrow. The danger will be during the judgment days. If Conchobor attends, you will have to miss observing them this year."

She was on the verge of dismissing me, halfway to her next task, when she turned back.

"And Finscoth," she cautioned, "your old name must not be uttered here. By the gods we honor, make sure the other girls are careful about that."

CHAPTER 25
CUCHULAINN'S DAUGHTER

The hardest part was not looking. I was glad Cathbad had not come, for the need to speak with him would have been a constant temptation. Even so, to keep my eyes averted through that long evening was a trial. What familiar faces had come from Emain Macha? Had Maeve traveled from Cruachan to answer Lugaid's summons? The desire gnawed at me to look on the woman—she with her crimson cloak and long yellow hair—who had brought about my father's downfall. And I longed to see if Berach stood in Lugaid's honor guard. But I did not long to see Conchobor, and so I kept my head down, attended to my duties and strove to be invisible.

We had no guests from other lands that night. It is the druids' duty to deal with the Otherworld; it is our duty likewise to shield the people from its perils. On the Isle of Women we seek out the fair ones who wander our world, for such is our training and our craft. But the Samhain rites on the Hill of Tlachta, and on other hills all over Ireland, are not only a re-enactment of the sun's decline and return; they also weave a spell of protection to rebuff the spirits who come through the veil on this night.

I had seen Tlachta in her feathered robe, of course, on the isle. Our lives there are punctuated by ritual and, except for the daily song to greet the sun's rising and setting, every sacred or ceremonial function requires the robes of office. But to see her there, in front of the most powerful kings of Ireland, set above the druids of the high king himself! My heart was full of pride when she stepped forth and raised her arms to command the crowd's attention. Though she was shortest of the Wise Ones assembled there, and a woman, in this she was counted greatest. And she was flawless, her voice ringing with power and assurance, her movements fluid and hypnotic. I could almost see the life force streaming into her from earth, sky, trees and water, so that she seemed to grow in stature and tower before the fire, commanding the attention of every eye.

It was a long night for the apprentices, for after all the kings and spectators had gone to their tents we stayed up and tended the fire, ensuring it did not die out until the first light of dawn. And so I rose late, after only a few hours of sleep, to the bustle of a camp being struck. The judgments would be held at Tara, where the high king's guests could be housed in comfort, and everywhere I looked tents were being collapsed, horses packed, cook fires extinguished. I needed to pack up as well. Tlachta had found a guide to take me to Roisin's house after everyone else had departed for Tara, and the four full days we would have together took the sting out of having to miss the high court. Still it galled me to be left behind. I pulled my cloak tighter against the chill and thought how strange it would feel to be the only person left on that sacred hill.

The stream was crowded; servants rinsed out cook pots and watered horses while a few late risers woke their faces up in its cold waters. That had been my thought too, but a wash would have to wait. The chance of being recognized was too great.

No one came near the druids' tents though, not without an

invitation. I pulled up my hood and ambled over to the handful of sleepy apprentices hunkered around a fire. Judging by the smell wafting from their iron pot, I was just in time for breakfast.

"Luaine!"

The word was shrieked out, knifing through the noise of the camp like a spear cast by Cuchulainn himself.

I swear by all the gods of my people, nobody can part a crowd like Roisin. Here she came, black hair flying, pregnant belly outlined against her cloak and men and horses alike all but jumping out of her way. She hurtled into me, and there I was, hugging the same old Roisin with a different body, the taut bulge of a baby about halfway to being born pressing against me.

Oh, and it was lovely to see her.

"I couldn't wait," she laughed, breathless from her run. "I got the message that you were coming, and I thought, why not ride out to meet you? It's certain you would end up on the wrong road without me to guide you!"

She straightened and gave me a critical eye. "You look barely awake. Are you only after rising now, then? I didn't realize the druid life was one of sloven and sloth."

I wonder if I will always cry and laugh together when I see Roisin. She and Berach are the only people left to me from my first life. Like Fintan, they bridge my past and my present. And however happy I am with my life now, there is still, I suppose, a loneliness for what was lost. Roisin awakens my memories.

"For the love of the goddess, let me fix your hair!" demanded Roisin, and I submitted happily, spooning in the porridge while she combed and braided and exclaimed over how smoky it smelled.

"That's Samhain smoke," I told her. "Breathe it with respect."

So there we were, joking and giddy and hanging off each other, lost in our news and gossip, when suddenly the dark hand in my belly clutched hard. I gasped with it, doubled over in pain, craning my head at the same time to try to see in every direction at once. This is it, I realized. I had thought the danger passed and safely avoided, but it was only now at my heels. And in my mind I heard again Roisin's voice, cutting like a clarion through the crowd. Her voice, shouting out my name.

"Luaine? What is it?" Roisin's hand was under my elbow, helping me to straighten, her face anxious with concern.

"Is the king still here, Roisin?"

"King Lugaid?" Bewilderment clouded her features. I forced a slow breath, curbing the urgency.

"Conchobor. Is Conchobor still here?"

Her fist came up to her mouth as she understood the situation. And that was when I saw Conchobor's standard, the fluttering colors of the Red Branch, marking the progress of the wedge of men riding toward us.

Ξ

The man who had stolen my lands and ordered me killed drew steadily nearer, and though I made myself stand tall, the fear was a live thing inside me. My mouth flooded with the taste of metal. I felt again the throbbing pain of my infected cheek, the fiery agony when Geanann cut away the rot. It was all I could do not to vomit.

Just as Conchobor dismounted, Tlachta appeared out of nowhere and calmly placed herself before me, a solid implacable bulk.

Conchobor strode over, looking like he meant to mow Tlachta down—but he did not. As though he had encountered an invisible wall, he came to an abrupt stop a good two feet from her.

He was red with anger, his pouched eyes glittering. Would he kill me himself, I wondered, on the spot? He had killed the poets in a fit of feigned outrage. He could accuse me of any wild thing, play the wounded righteous husband...

"Is there something I can help you with, King Conchobor?" If you dressed Tlachta in rags, her voice alone would mark her as druid. Respectful, calm, pleasant...and for all that it was, unmistakably, a voice filled with authority and laced with threat. A voice to remind Conchobor who it was that addressed him.

He is the King of Ulster, after all, and not so easily cowed. Still his manner changed, the explosive rage brought under control, the pale eyes turned calculating. I was not sure it was an improvement.

His eyes drilled into me, though he spoke to Tlachta.

"Why do you stand between a man and his wife? This is the Queen of Ulster, and her duty lies in Emain Macha. Luaine will return with me."

He bent all his heavy will into those words, and the armed honor guard ranged behind him was a persuasive reinforcement. I had no doubt he was willing to take me by force.

Tlachta's face was an impassive blank, giving away nothing.

"You are mistaken, my king. This is Finscoth, one of my apprentices. She is nothing to do with you."

Conchobor's veneer of civility dropped away then, and he began to rail at Tlachta, the spittle spraying from his mouth with the force of his outrage, his cheeks mottling with it. She simply remained planted before me, immovable as a tree.

Even trees can be felled, I thought, and even as I became alarmed for my Mistress I felt Roisin beside me, wired with tension, breast heaving, and I realized she was near to flying at the King of Ulster in my defense.

With that the paralyzing fear drained away from me, replaced by a cold resolve. No one would be hurt here on my behalf, nor would I hide any longer behind the skirts of my friends and teachers. I felt my chin lift and with it my strength. My hands, clenched almost into fists at my sides, touched and then curled around two objects—the hilt of my sword, and the pouch containing Liban's crystal that hung now at my side. A gift from my father. A gift from beyond. And I felt Emer's gifts, woven so deeply into my own fabric that there was no need for any token. The meaning and power of each gift hung in my mind. In that moment, Conchobor's bluster and Tlachta's cool replies faded to nothing, and I stood in a bubble of silent clarity.

From that clear place, I stepped directly in front of the king.

Ξ

The first time rage took hold of me, and I but a girl of twelve, it burned me with its heat. This time the anger was not fiery but freezing, cold as a dead man's blood. And this time the voice that spoke was my own.

I felt such contempt for this man it repelled me to look upon him. Yet I did. I stood very close, turned just enough that he was forced to look full upon the ruin he had made. I locked my eyes upon his as if it were two blue spears of ice I was aiming. And he must have felt them, for he stepped back a pace, his threats and curses frozen in his throat.

And then I spoke, very quietly, making him listen. I dropped the words into his mind like heavy stones in a pond.

"King Conchobor knows who I am."

I paused. Make him wait for it, I thought. My lips pulled into a smile that never reached my eyes—a smile that was very nearly an outright sneer.

"And I know what he is."

I took his measure as the implications of my words made themselves felt. Ripples spreading across the pond. He had not known he was discovered, I was sure of it. He had thought his secret dead and buried with the two poets in their burning house. I addressed him directly now.

"I am no longer Luaine. I am no longer your wife. I have left that life behind, and it would be well for you to do the same.

"For there are more than a few in this land who know what was done to me, and by whom. Do you think the men of Ulster will follow you still, when they hear of the treachery and greed that led you to betray the daughter of your best champion, and she a girl of tender years and blameless honor? Do you think the high king, who was beloved by my father, will long suffer your presence?"

I let the rocks sink into the water of his mind and watched the turbulence of his thoughts. Let him fear he might drown, before tossing him the line.

"Luaine is dead, mourned and gone. You have your wife's lands and herds. Do not seek for more. For however I am called, I will always be Cuchulainn's daughter. And I swear on his good name that if I am killed, I will do you more harm from the grave than I ever would in life."

I made my eyes frozen iron. I made the Truth of my words into a weight he could not shrug off. I held him. Old and powerful as he was, I held him.

And then I let him go.

Ξ

The surge of power left me shaky and sick as it drained away. I kept my legs until the last of Conchobor's men was gone from sight, and then they folded of their own accord to the ground.

Tlachta wrapped me in cloaks, found a fire still unquenched and sat with me while my strength slowly returned. As she tended me, she alternately scolded me for overextending myself so recklessly, and beamed with pride at what I had managed. Eventually, though, she became aware that Roisin glowered at her with a recklessness of her own.

"The sick feeling will pass," Tlachta told me. "And I imagine it will pass all the sooner if I remove myself from between two long-parted friends."

"You leave me in the best of hands," I told her. "There is no one could look after me better, as she has already proven." The glower transformed itself into a smile nearly as sunny as Geanann's.

I went home with Roisin, and her house with Berach was as bright and brisk and comfortable as I had imagined. But I went to the judgments too and heard the cases, for my days of hiding were over. And if Conchobor was there also, it was no concern of mine.

I was free of him.

And though he was also free of me and grasped my lands in

his hand with none to gainsay him, yet I almost pitied him. I still do. For the days of his life run short, and when his time comes to pass through the veil into the next life, I know what awaits him there.

The Hound will have him. And the Hound will have no pity.

EPILOGUE

I have one last thing to tell you before we part ways. It concerns Geanann's last visit to the isle.

It had been a year since I had seen him, and I felt awkward in his presence as I never had before. Living with women as I did, I thought little of my appearance and had barely noticed the changes that had steadily transformed my angular girl's frame into a woman's body. Now, though, as he sat so near to me, I was aware of the thrust of my breasts against my shift as if they had sprung out overnight, and I could not find a way to sit that did not seem to display them. And when he rolled back his sleeves to catch the cooling breeze, the sight of the golden hair glinting on the swell of his forearm was such a distraction to me I could hardly follow his words.

You will be laughing at me now, I am sure. A young woman taken with a man, and so cut off from her own heart she could not see the obvious!

But I could not let myself see. Not with a purple track carved down my face that ensured no man would ever be taken with me. I had not been long recovered from that wound when I determined that the only way to deal with such a thing was to keep a firm leash on my own heart and to be content with the love between friends.

And I managed it too. I tore my eyes from the strong hands, the bright smile, and concentrated on his words, and gradually the self-consciousness left me and I was once again at ease. And we traded news of our lives like old friends: Geanann's travels and adventures and his testing soon to come, my studies and my growing interest in the law.

And then I told him of the name Tlachta had given me on Samhain. I shook my head.

"I am getting used to it. I like that my name is linked to Fintan's—it speaks to the bond between us. But really. White Blossom? It is a name for a woman of great beauty, not—"

"Then it is a name for you."

Startled, I could not stop my eyes from finding his, and there was something in their gray depths that held me. As if in protest, my hand rose to cover the scar—but Geanann reached out and caught my wrist and pulled it down.

"Don't. You need never hide that from me. What do you think I see when I look at that scar that I made myself, though it was the hardest thing I ever had to do? It's a young girl's courage I see, courage to shame a warrior. And Luaine—Finscoth—I see a woman's beauty shining through it, so bright it nearly blinds me."

He had never loosed his hold on my wrist, and he pulled gently on it now, leaning forward to take my head in his other hand. He put his lips just under my eye where the scar began and he slowly traced its length, over the swell of my cheekbone to the point of my jaw. And by the time he arrived at its end I was lost. He did not have to search for my lips—I could no more have kept them from him than stop my own breath. And for a long time there were no words between us, for it was a different language altogether we were speaking.

"It is so long I have been dreaming of that kiss." His smile washed over me, and I basked shamelessly in it. It made me happy just to look at his face, and it was a wonder to me that his eyes lingered over my features with the same delight.

"How long?" I had had no idea.

"Oh, now… These things creep up on a person unawares. But I believe it may have been the day you jumped on your horse and galloped off without me, and your wound barely set."

"Why did you wait to tell me, then? I was old enough." Even as I said the words I knew they were untrue. I may have been old enough, but I had not been ready.

Geanann was shaking his head. "I wanted your love freely given," he said. "You were so alone and so young. I was afraid you might feel I was demanding repayment. Worse, I was afraid you might feel compelled to give it."

"But I am old enough now," I said, and this time I didn't get his light-up-the-world smile but a smoldering look that sparked a rising heat in my belly.

"Oh yes," he said softly. "You are old enough now."

☰

He left the next morning, with a promise to return to me soon.

"We have much to talk about," he said seriously, "but it is hard now to talk when you are by me."

I smiled—a part of me still dazed to find myself trading lovers' jokes—but I knew he was right. It was not so simple between us, not if I was to continue my training. And that, Geanann had made clear, he would not interrupt. "You have only started to discover your gifts," he said, "and while, if the gods are with me,

I will be resplendent in feathers the next time you see me, I am not qualified to take an apprentice. Even if I were, I could not match the richness of learning you have here."

But I didn't fret over it. I was learning to trust my path. If we were meant to be together, a way would reveal itself.

At the causeway, Geanann held me tight and kissed me one last time. I threaded my arms around his neck and let the world fall away. And then I watched him ride onto the mainland and disappear down the road.

I could hear the whispers and giggles behind me. There are some thirty women on the isle, druidesses, apprentices and servants, and by the time I returned to my studies there would not be one who had not heard about me and Geanann. I didn't mind. One of Roisin's down-to-earth homilies came to mind: A man who proclaims his love before witnesses is a man who will stand by his word. It would be long before we could marry, but we would pledge to each other at Beltane all the same.

So much of life is a mystery, hidden even from the wisest. I had not looked for love, but it found me all the same. And it made me think again on Emer and Cuchulainn, and on the love that was between them.

I understand my mother's choice better now. Her life with Cuchulainn had blazed like a bright flame. It must have seemed to her that what remained after his death was a spark so faint and feeble it was not worth the tending. Better to go out together. And yet…our lives are a gift from the gods. As long as the light still glows within us, no matter how faint, should we be so quick to stamp it out?

It takes courage to die in battle, or to take one's own life as my mother did. But it takes courage to live as well: to face the long black nights of grief, to rise from the ashes and begin again. To trust that like the warmth of spring or the light from the Samhain fire, happiness may yet return.

I have so much to learn. But some things I have learned, not least about who I am. As I turned back from the causeway and returned to the island that has become my home, a triad came to me. The words sounded in my head like a heartbeat, and I knew them to be true. They are three petals on the white blossom I am cultivating within me. I wake to the knowledge of them every day:

My name is Finscoth.

I follow the druid's path.

I am loved.

FICTION AND MYTH

Like most writers who have tried to turn a legend into a modern novel, I have taken liberties with my source material. This is not, as I heard one writer accused of, an arrogant attempt to make the myth into what I think it should have been, but rather to adapt it as the backdrop for a coherent, emotionally engaging story for a modern reader.

So, true confession time for some of my worst sins:

First, my heroine. The best-known sagas don't mention any daughter of Cuchulainn and Emer, though I did come across one reference to Finscoth, who is listed as Cuchulainn's daughter in *Names from Myths and Legends* prepared by Bruce L. Jones. However, no other heroes' young children are named in the sagas either—I assume because they were not germane to the action, not because they did not exist. So it's a fair bet that Cuchulainn and Emer could have had a child, and since Cuchulainn's son by Aoife is referred to as his "only" son, any other offspring would have been female.

Luaine, who was betrothed or married to Conchobor and then beset by Aithirne and his sons, is said in various versions to be the daughter of a chieftain of the Sidhe, or of a low-profile fellow named Domanchenn. And she dies from the satirists' attack. I have made her Cuchulainn's daughter, rescued her and invented a reason for her true identity to have been suppressed.

The story of Cuchulainn's many wounds in the battle for the bull of Cooley, and his strange sleep and subsequent visit with the Otherworld woman, Fand, are based on two separate incidents which I have blended into one.

The food-poisoning disaster at Dun Lethglaise I have made up, but it is inspired by an existing story of Cuchulainn's anger at not being told of a feast (held by one Conall mac Gleo Ghlais), and a remark by Maeve, who insists her invasion will go well since not only are the Ulstermen stricken by the pangs of Macha, but one-third of them are up with Celthair in Dun Lethglaise. The pangs of Macha were a curse dating even farther back in history than Cuchulainn's day, consigning the men of Ulster to the pains of a woman in labor at the time they were most beset by enemies.

Last, but not least, I have rather unfairly made Conchobor into a villain. There is plenty of evidence that his attitude toward women left something to be desired by today's standards, but no suggestion that he actually engineered Luaine's death.

WHO'S WHO—AND HOW TO SAY IT

Note: "kh" is pronounced as a soft "k" in the back of the throat.

Abhartach (AWV-ar-tokh) Aithirne's son, a poet

Ailill (AL-il) King of Connaught

Aithirne (ATH-ir-na) Poet

Alba (AWL-ba) Present-day Scotland/Wales

Aoife (EE-fa) Warrior queen of Alba; mother of Conlaoch

Baile's Strand (BOLL-ya) Beach near Dun Dealgan

Baire (BAR-ra) Conchobor's ally

Ban drui (BAHN-dree) Female druid

Beltane (BYAL-tun-a) Spring festival—May 1; return of the light

Berach (BER-akh) Cuchulainn's master at arms and Luaine's trainer

Bricriu (BRIK-ru) Poet

Brocc (BRUK) Roisin's father

Bronach (BRO-nakh) Apprentice on Isle of Women

Cathbad (CAW-vud) Chief Druid of Ulster

Ceara (KYAR-a) Emer's horse

Celthair (KEL-thar) Host of feast where warriors are poisoned

Cluain-na-mBan (CLOON-na-MON) Isle of Women; presently Our Lady's Island

Conall Cearnach (CON-al CAR-nokh) Warrior; avenges Cuchulainn

Conchobor (CON-kh-vur) King of Ulster; Cuchulainn's uncle

Conlaoch (CON-laykh) Cuchulainn's son by Aoife

Connaught (Con-AWT) Province of Ireland

Cooley Mountains (as written) Low mountain range just north of Dun Dealgan

Cruachan (CROO-khan) Connaught's Royal Seat

Cuchulainn (Coo-KHULL-in) Luaine's father

Cuingedach (KWING-a-dukh) Aithirne's son, a poet

Cu Roi (Coo Roy) King of Munster; powerful druid

Cuscraid (COO-crid) Conchobor's son

Daigh (DAY) Druid who presides over Luaine's coming of age

Damnhait (DAV-nit) Apprentice on Isle of Women

Deirdriu (DARE-dru) Conchobor's wife

Donn Cooley (as written) Ulster's great brown bull

Dun Dealgan (DOON DYAL-gan) Luaine's first home

Dun Lethglaise (DOON LAY-GLASH-a) Celthair's house; site of food-poisoning

Eirnin (ER-neen) Luaine's tutor

Emain Macha (EV-in MOKH-a) Ulster's Royal Seat

Emer (AY-ver) Luaine's mother

Eoghan (OH-en) Warrior who kills Naoise

Fand (FOND) Woman of the Sidhe; loves Cuchulainn

Ferdia (FAR-dee-ah) Cuchulainn's friend; fights for Connaught

Fergus (FER-gus) Trusted warrior; defects to Connaught

Fidchell (FID-chull) Game similar to chess

Fili (FEEL-y) Seer

Fingin (FIN-gwin) Conchobor's healer

Finnbennach (FIN-ba-nokh) Connaught's mighty white bull

Finnchad (FIN-khad) Conchobor's son

Finscoth (FIN-scot) Luaine's new name

Fintan (FIN-tan) Luaine's raven

Follaman (FOLL-a-vun) Conchobor's son

Forgall (FOR-gul) Emer's father

Gae Bolga (Guh BOLL-ga) Cuchulainn's notched spear

Geanann (GA-nawn) Cathbad's son; druid and healer

Geasa (GEES-a) Taboos

Laeg (LOYG) Cuchulainn's charioteer

Laegaire (LAYR-a) Ulster warrior

Lasair (LA-sar) Cuchulainn's poet; Luaine's teacher

Leinster (LEN-ster) Province of Ireland

Liban (LEE-ban) Woman of the Sidhe

Luaine (LOO-in-ya) Cuchulainn's daughter

Lugaid of the Red Stripes (LOO-ad); New High King at Tara

Lugh (LOO) God of sun and fine craftsmanship; rumored to be Cuchulainn's father

Lughaid (LOO-ee) Warrior of Connaught

Lughnasadh (LOO-na-sa) Harvest festival—Aug. 1; named for god Lugh

Macha (MAW-kha) Master druid on the Isle of Women

Maeve (MAVE) Queen of Connaught

Manannan (MON-an-an) God of the sea

Miach (MEE-akh) Sencha's wife

Morrigu, The (MOR-ee-goo) Goddess of war and discord

Mug Ruith (MUG RITH) A sun god

Muireann (MWIR-in) Apprentice on the Isle of Women

Muirthemne (Mur-HEV-na) Area around Dun Dealgan

Munster (MUN-ster) Province of Ireland

Naoise (NEE-sha) Deirdriu's lover

Neeth (as written) River near Dun Dealgan

Niall (NEE-ul) Horse master

Ochain (UH-khan) Conchobor's magic shield

Ogham (OH-am or OG-am) Ancient writing system

Orlagh (OR-la) Luaine's horse

Osnait (OS-naid) Emer's maid

Rathnait (RATH-nit) Teacher on the Isle of Women

Roisin (RO-sheen) Luaine's maid

Rosnaree (Russ-na-REE) Battle site

Samhain (SAHV-in) First day of winter—Nov. 1; Celtic New Year

Saraid (SAWR-ud) Apprentice on the Isle of Women

Scathach (SKAW-thakh) Female Scottish warrior; Cuchulainn's teacher

Seanan (SHAN-awn) Celthair's groom

Sencha (SHEN-kha) Conchobor's peacemaker

Setanta (SHAY-dan-da) Cuchulainn's birth name

Sidhe (SHEE) The Tuatha de Danaan (see below)

Sualtim (SOO-al-div) Cuchulainn's father

Tara (TAR-a) High king's royal seat

Tlachta (TLOKH-ta) Chief Druid on the Isle of Women

Tomman (TUM-un) Roisin's brother

Torc (TURK) Decorative neck ring

Treasa (TRASS-a) First level druid on the Isle of Women

Tuatha da Danaan (TOO-ah-tha DAY DAH-nan) An immortal race skilled in
    enchantments who live in a realm normally invisible to humans

Tullia (TULL-ya) Luaine's nurse

Uath (OO-ah) Cu-Roi's enchanted disguise

Ulster (UL-ster) Province of Ireland

Holly Bennett is the author of *The Bonemender*, *The Bonemender's Oath* and the forthcoming *The Gray Veil*, all published by Orca. In her "real" life she works as editor-in-chief of *Today's Parent* Special Editions. Born in Montreal, she lives in Peterborough, Ontario, with a houseful of musicians (three sons and husband John) and a nice quiet dog.